"Help! I'm Being Held Prisoner."

Luke took Georgia into his arms, and his mouth came down on hers in the timeless way men have of silencing women instantly. The kiss was devastating! Her body went mad. Her bones melted; her blood turned to fire; her mouth gave up. She was absolutely shameless. Slowly, her free hand went up to the back of his head, and she leaned her body into his as her mind departed for parts unknown.

When Luke lifted his mouth and looked down into her face, his eyes were smoldering. She lay back on his arm, waiting for more.

He said in a low voice, "You said you wouldn't say a word."

"You fight dirty."

"You try yelling for help again and see what you get."

Dear Reader,

Happy summertime reading from all of us here at Silhouette! As the days of summer wind to an end, take the time to curl up with August's wonderful love stories. These are books as hot as the most sizzling summer's day!

We start with Mary Lynn Baxter's *Man of the Month* novel *Tall in the Saddle,* which has a hero you'll never forget—Flint Carson, a man as rugged and untamed as the land he ranches. This is a book you'll want to read over and over again. It's a keeper!

Also in August comes a wild, witty romp from Lass Small, *The Molly Q.* Don't ask me to explain; I'll just say it has to do with computers, kidnapping and marvelous fun.

Rounding out August is *A Wolf in Sheep's Clothing,* a tie-in to July's *Never Tease a Wolf*—both by the talented Joan Johnston. And don't miss books from Naomi Horton, Ryanne Corey and Sally Goldenbaum. Each and every Silhouette Desire novel this month is one that I am keeping in my personal library.

So go wild with Desire—you'll be glad you did.

All the best,

Lucia Macro
Senior Editor

LASS
SMALL
THE MOLLY Q

SILHOUETTE *Desire*®

Published by Silhouette Books New York

America's Publisher of Contemporary Romance

SILHOUETTE BOOKS
300 East 42nd St., New York, N.Y. 10017

THE MOLLY Q

ISBN: 0-373-05655-9

First Silhouette Books printing August 1991

Printed in the U.S.A.

Books by Lass Small

Silhouette Desire

Tangled Web #241
To Meet Again #322
Stolen Day #341
Possibles #356
Intrusive Man #373
To Love Again #397
Blindman's Bluff #413
Goldilocks and the Behr #437
Hide and Seek #453
Red Rover #491
Odd Man Out #505
Tagged #534
Contact #548
Wrong Address, Right Place #569
Not Easy #578
The Loner #594
Four Dollars and Fifty-One Cents #613
No Trespassing Allowed #638
The Molly Q #655

Silhouette Romance

An Irritating Man #444
Snow Bird #521

Silhouette Books

Silhouette Christmas Stories 1989
"Voice of the Turtles"

LASS SMALL

finds that living on this planet at this time is a fascinating experience. People are amazing. She thinks that to be a teller of tales of people, places and things is absolutely marvelous.

One

Moving from Cleveland to Indianapolis was no big deal. Even her travel expenses were being paid by the courier service. Georgia Brown Baines glanced briefly down at the modest brown envelope under her purse on the passenger seat of her car.

The courier service had cautioned Georgia not to allow anyone to see its address or to mention the receiving company's name. As they'd enclosed it in the anonymous brown envelope, they'd said it had to be in Indianapolis by evening. No sweat. She'd have it there by that afternoon.

All her worldly goods, plus her cat, were packed into her little pink car. Pink. When she could manage, she would have to have it painted. Pink was noticeable. But she had worked for a florist, and she had made unscheduled deliveries, so painting the car pink had seemed appropriate. When Georgia was involved with anything, she threw herself into it without restraint. She was loyal.

The only thing she hadn't liked about her job at the flower shop had been her boss. He'd wanted to make her bloom, too. Georgia had demurred, and he hadn't appreciated the geranium plant she'd used to decorate his head. She was still sorry the geranium had been in a plastic pot. A clay pot smashing over his wicked, pointed little head would have been more satisfying.

Her green-eyed black cat made an inquiring mew and came up onto the front seat to put her paws on the dashboard to survey the traffic.

"So, Minny, what do you think of all the cars running around like mechanical mice?" she asked as they went along Highway 70 through Indy before going to the west side of the city by the airport.

Minny yawned and dropped back to the seat on top of Georgia's coach purse, which was on top of the mysterious envelope. The cat watched as Georgia guided the car, then blinked slowly in boredom.

Georgia wasn't unfamiliar with Indianapolis. It was the home of the Indy 500. It was a marvelous city, with its Monument Circle. The arts were cherished and made available to the citizens with great flair. And there was the Hoosier Dome.

It was a hot day in early August. The air was humid with the threat of storms. Her car wasn't air-conditioned, and her orange shirtwaist stuck to her back as sweat trickled under her arms and between her breasts.

Georgia was attractive and deliberately slender. Her shoulder-length hair was soft and a shiny brown, while her eyes were a strange hazel. She was a confident woman, twenty-eight years old. She was two years a widow.

That being a widow had caused problems. As the florist had insisted, "It's nothing you ain't had before. Just better." How could a *florist* be so crude?

Having taken the access road to Highway 465 and now driving an adjusted north, Georgia watched for signs of the Montana Electronics Company, Inc. and finally saw it. She turned off at the highway exit, followed that road and found the company parking lot. At the gate she told the suspicious attendant, "I'm hand-delivering a courier letter to Luke Montana."

The gatekeeper had to get clearance, and as he phoned from his booth he watched her like a hawk. Her, her snooty cat and her packed pink car.

He came back to her car window and said doubtfully, "You can put your car over there in the shade of the building, but don't be more than half an hour."

"Minny thanks you for the shade."

"Minny?" He looked at the cat skeptically. "She know about Minnie Mouse?"

"Incessantly. The name was a mad impulse when she was very, very small."

"We got a kid named Albatross. It seemed funny until he caught on, then we worried. Good thing he didn't mind. But he calls himself Ross."

Georgia returned his grin and shook hands with another human whose humor was a bit different. Easing away to park as she'd been directed, she left Minny in the car with the windows open several inches. Georgia took the mysterious envelope and her purse, then walked to the entrance, where she had to ring a bell for admittance.

Standing, waiting, she wondered what product they made that their security was so intense? She had to identify herself and show her driver's license, but they didn't ask to see her moles or scars.

Apparently hand-delivered letters to Luke Montana weren't unusual, because no one questioned that she needed to wait until she could actually give the letter to him. On the unimaginative, pristine second floor, the serious receptionist showed Georgia into an empty conference room as she said, "It will be only a minute. Would you like coffee?"

"May I have a drink of water?"

The receptionist replied a calm: "Of course."

Georgia waited, alone, in the empty room. Along with her excessive imagination, she was a little claustrophobic. There were no windows. There was a skylight and indirect lighting. On the far wall was a picture of a stern man who glowered at her. Chairs had been placed around an oval table which held an empty pitcher on a tray with glasses that had been turned upside-down. And there was a telephone.

If no one came for her, she could use the phone to call for help. How would the police get inside to find her? A SWAT team would figure it out. It was their job to help citizens held in windowless rooms against their will.

The opposite door opened with a snap and she jerked around. The intruder was a sinfully gorgeous man, a little older than she, and he was apparently just as startled at seeing her. He stood there for a minute not saying anything, and she stared back at him. He appeared to fill the room. His presence had that impact.

The intruder was taller than her five feet six inches by over another half foot. His dark hair was thick and not quite tidy and his oddly compelling eyes were almost yellow brown. His brows were thick and straight, his lashes a surprise. His nose had been broken and he looked tough. He would have looked tough if his nose hadn't been broken.

He was built in a formidable wedge and wore his clothes easily, but he would be as confident and as impressive in no clothes at all. In a room full of people, in a crisis, everyone would look to him to solve it . . . and he would.

"Ms. Baines?" His voice curled around her nerve ends and made them vibrate, so that she couldn't reply right away. "You have a letter for me?" He prompted her.

"Uh..." She continued to stare and she felt heat rise in her. Of course the heat was from the August day and from her embarrassment at standing there in that rumpled, sweat-drenched, awful orange shirtwaist dress. And her hair was a mess and she'd chewed off all her lipstick. She knew that she looked absolutely ghastly.

"Oh, sorry," the intruder said quickly. He smiled slightly, as a man does for a woman who attracts him. "I'm Luke Montana." And he took out his wallet to show his identification.

She thought he meant to tip her, so she hastened to say, "They paid me." And she put out a hand to stop him from giving her money.

"What? Who paid you? Why?"

"For the letter."

"You sold the letter?" He showed considerable shock. "You couldn't possibly do anything like that."

"To deliver it."

"Where?"

"Here." It was a strange conversation.

"This is the letter? A copy? How very thoughtful." But his voice was dangerous.

"Good grief! This is the *only* letter. I didn't sell it. This isn't a copy. It's the letter I was told to deliver to you. And I'm hours early getting here! This whole outfit is paranoid! And I thought Melvin was hyper."

"You didn't sell out to Herb?" He tore open the covering plain brown envelope and took the actual letter into his hands. It was sealed and there were even wax blobs on the flap.

"Who is Herb?" she asked.

"It's sealed."

"Of course, it's sealed." She looked around. She was alone in that windowless room with a suspected madman. A formidable, attractive one, but nevertheless a madman. Attractiveness doesn't cancel out total madness. Such an affliction only made the flaw all the more regrettable.

"Stay here. I'll be right back." He strode to the hall door.

"I need a drink of water."

"Right." He opened the door and exited, closing it after him.

There she stood. There wasn't even canned music. Just she was there in that prison room, the helpless captive of an attractive maniac, and without even a drink of water. There had to be a water fountain around somewhere.

Georgia went to the hall door and turned the knob. It didn't turn. The door was locked. She tried to rat-

tle it and it wasn't rattleable. They'd accidentally
locked her in there? Or had it been deliberate?

She turned, aghast, and lay a calming hand on her
rounded chest as she leaned back against the door. She
really was locked into that room. She really was a
prisoner?

*Now, Georgia, in real life people don't do this sort
of thing to other people.* Oh, yes. It's in the paper
every day. *Every day?* Almost.

If she stood on the table and put a chair on it and
climbed up on that, could she get out of the skylight?
It was probably sealed, and her shoe heel wouldn't
break it. She looked around for a tool to unseal the
skylight and her glance fell on the unobtrusive handle
of the door through which Luke Montana had entered. Was it also locked?

She went over and hesitantly reached for the handle. It lifted smoothly, and the door swung slowly
open. *The Lady or the Tiger?* Which would it be. She
watched as it opened, breathing through her mouth in
some suspense. A bacchanalia? She moved her head
to get the first peek through the door's crack.

Revealed was a very nice office. No one was in it.
She slipped through the door and looked around. It
had windows. There was the usual office furniture, a
big, lush plant that could also use some water, closed
double doors into the hall and a smaller door in the
opposite wall.

She went to the smaller one and pushed it open to
find a closet/bath. There was a cup dispenser and she
finally got a drink of water.

She refilled the cup and walked back into the office
to stand at the window looking out. To the south,
there was productive rolling Indiana countryside. To

the southwest, on the horizon, were some threatening clouds. She turned toward the room and saw an elaborate blueprint spread on the top of the desk with a blue folder marked "Molly Q." Molly Q? That sounded like a ship. Not a very big one. More like a riverboat or somebody's weekend boat.

She heard an exclamation from the conference room. Next, the connecting door was flung back. And Luke Montana stood there a minute, his stare on Georgia.

Then he blinked and said, "Uh . . ." And after that he asked, "What are you doing in here?" He looked around, then appeared to reach a decision. He strode strongly into the room and reached a square hand over the desk, quickly folded over the blueprints and punched a button. "Mac, get in here! We've got a problem."

A little irritated, Georgia asked, "What in the world?"

"Who sent you?" he snapped. His yellow eyes smoldered as they went over her.

"The courier service." She enunciated through her teeth, leaning slightly forward from her waist. Then she straightened and sipped more of the water.

"But you took the first opportunity to snoop around," he reminded her. He was somewhat intimidating.

"I was thirsty. I'd asked the receptionist for a drink of water, but apparently, since it wasn't coffee, she was stumped. And the hall door was *locked!*"

"Understandably. I should have locked this door, too!"

"I was not snooping." She spaced the words as if chiding Minny.

"What did you see?" His voice was extremely deep and attractive.

"You have a nice office. It has windows." She was quite pleased she could give him a cool glance.

A man came in one of the double doors from the hall. He, too, stopped cautiously and stood still as if to prevent her from any attempt to escape past him into the hall. It caused a squiggle of alarm in her that they should consider that she might want to escape them.

The new arrival was almost as tall as Luke and looked as if he'd played only a reasonable amount of pro-football and could still move without undue pain. His hair was thinning, his color was healthy and he hadn't gone to flab. He was watching her.

Luke asked Georgia sternly, "What have you seen?"

"The blueprints?" She guessed with some parsimonious humor. It didn't take a genius to figure that out.

The two men exchanged a quick glance.

"About what?" Luke's voice was hard.

She shrugged. "Something about the Molly Q?" She guessed that.

"Ah-hah!" In an aside to Mac, he said, "We'll have to keep her."

"But how can we handle that?" Mac wanted to know in shock.

"We will. One word about the Molly Q, and he'll know."

"I'm not at all sure—" Mac began to protest in a calming way.

"She saw the blueprints." Luke gave him a hard stare.

"Well, yes, but—"

Luke said pithily, "The blueprints are the whole."

Mac blinked slowly twice and then stared. "The blueprints?"

Georgia warned. "I don't know what this is all about, but—"

"We'll only need to keep you for a week. Ten days at the most." Luke looked at her with slightly narrowed eyes.

"What are you talking about?" She really was in the middle of madmen!

"You understand perfectly, if you know the Molly Q."

She guessed, "It's a riverboat?"

"Cute." He acted as if he didn't think it was anywhere near to cute. "What's in the folder?"

"Look, Mr. Montana, I didn't look in the folder. I only glanced at the name before I saw the blueprints."

"Maybe we shouldn't—" Mac watched Luke.

But Luke asked, "What do you remember about the blueprints? Be serious about this. It's very important to us. And I swear to you, on my honor, we won't harm you in any way. What do you remember?"

"They're in blue." She was out of patience.

"This is deadly serious. *What do you remember?*"

She closed her eyes. "A center with radiating corridors..." she said musingly, then she opened her eyes.

Luke's perfect mouth tightened as he contemplated the problem, and he turned to Mac. "She's got it. That's all Herb would need."

"What?" She frowned.

Mac rubbed his mouth.

Luke said to Mac, "She gets back to Herb—"

Mac nodded and finished it: "—we're dead."

"I don't know what *any* of this is about!" she protested.

"You know too much." Luke was resigned to it.

"Are you planning…to…to do something rash with me? You do remember crime doesn't pay? Murder will out?" Her voice squeaked as she backed to the window. Would she kill herself if she jumped from the second floor, or only break her legs and not be able to run? What would happen to Minny?

Luke was explaining, "We just have to keep you away from Herb for ten days."

"Who is Herb?" It seemed a logical question to her.

"Don't think we're stupid," Luke told her levelly. "He sent you here."

"If he calls, we could say she's had an emergency appendectomy. She can't just disappear." Mac was leaning against the hall door with his arms folded, his face blank as he considered the possibilities.

"Disappear?" she whispered.

"We are civilized." Luke gave her a weighing look. "Even with little snoops."

"It would help if I knew what I'm supposed to know," she said impatiently.

"You want even more information?" Luke inquired with almost amused sarcasm. "How about the cost estimates?"

Mac said thoughtfully, "We'll have to think of something. Herb will raise Cain if she just disappears. He'd know she knew something and he'd raise hell trying to find her to find out what she knows."

"I know *nothing!*" She declared that stridently.

"Too much." Luke shook his head sadly.

Mac contributed: "How about if she calls him?"

Luke shook his head. "How do we know they haven't a code?"

Mac nodded. "With all there is at stake, he probably thought we might catch her snooping."

"But I don't know *anything!*" Georgia repeated, yet again.

Luke wasn't listening to her. "He'd have her hypnotized, and she'd spill the whole thing. She probably has total recall."

"Women are like that," Mac agreed with a mournful shake of his head. "They remember niggling little things from *years* ago!"

Luke gave Georgia a contemplative look. "How much would you take not to talk? To just leave the country?"

"I do think you must be crazy," she began, then added quickly, "Oh, I am sorry! You're not supposed to say that to anyone who isn't in control. I forgot."

Luke was still watching her. There were golden fires in his strange yellow-brown eyes. "I wish you could forget."

"Yeah," Mac added regretfully. "Some day we'll be able to reach in and smooth out memory."

Georgia gasped, "Why, that's perfectly awful!"

Luke moved his gorgeous body tiredly and she almost missed his comment. "What about lifting out the memory from someone who's been through a really bad experience and can't get over it? Can't face living with it?"

"Yes." She could certainly see that . . . like Phillip's death.

His look held some humor. "Or a little snoop who's seen something she had no business seeing?"

Mac was still on his own track. "We'll have to wait for Herb to get in touch and play it by ear."

"When did you say you'd report back?" Luke asked her, and his eyes went down her body.

"I didn't!" She frowned at him.

"How will he know when you're finished here?"

"I'll have delivered the letter. Then presumably you will call him, to tell him it's here. You will then learn he doesn't know me from Adam—or rather Eve—and I shall leave!" She instructed idiots. "So call him and get this cleared up. The parking lot attendant gave me a half hour to park my car in the shade and my cat is out there all this time. I have to leave!"

"Not now, you don't get away. And you must know Herb didn't write the letter."

"I believe you are cr— This is a very strange situation, and it wasn't covered at Ohio State University."

Luke nodded. Then he sat one hip on the corner of his desk and asked her, "We want to know, what were your instructions from Herb? He would have considered the possibility that you might get caught. What sort of code did he figure out for you to let him know you've hit the jackpot?"

"Who is Herb?" She flung out both hands in exasperation.

"Don't try to kid us," Luke warned.

"I don't know this…Herb, and all I was told to do was to deliver that letter. Which I did!"

"Where'll we keep her?" Mac asked.

"Your place?"

"Penny is a love, but she can't keep a secret. You know that. How would I explain all this to her? Do you think for one minute our secret guest is going to be aloof? She'd tell Penny everything. Everybody spills their guts to Penny. She'll tell Penny, and Penny will help her escape! Then she'll get to Herb and the . . . butter will hit the fan."

"True." Luke ran a careless hand through his thick hair. "How about Karen?"

"Pete is not to be trusted around any female over fourteen."

There was a silence. The two men's eyes met, and Luke sighed. "My place."

"The only solution." Mac comforted him.

"No." By then, Georgia knew in her bones that Luke was not married. It was bad enough being in the same room with him under tense, slightly hostile circumstances. If she was alone with him at his apartment? No way. She would be bemused by him and, since he thought she was a corporate pirate, he might consider that she was fair game and— There is a limit to how much a body could resist.

What made her think he was attracted? Why would he be interested in her body in that rumpled orange dress? Dotted with black cat hair? With her own hair in a tangle? And no makeup on?

"She'll just have to stay at my place." Luke's deep voice was thrilling to her core.

"Who'll you get for guard?" Mac asked.

"You."

Mac laughed. "With Penny? A football groupie, radar wife? You jest."

Luke accepted the responsibility. "Me."

"Yep." Mac agreed.

"No!" Georgia dissented.

Luke gave her a gleaming yellow-fire look. "Little girls who play with fire, get burned."

That's what worried her.

Luke indicated a chair to Georgia. "You might as well sit down. We can't leave until the place is empty. Relax. You look like a green-eyed doe cornered by two hounds."

She didn't touch that one. She hesitated then decided to pretend to cooperate. She sat down on the edge of one chair. She soothed her orange shirt over her knees, as if it was the material that was nervous and she kept a calming hand on it, but her mind was clicking away like mad. "My cat," she blurted.

Both men looked at her strangely.

"My cat, Minny, is out in the car in this heat."

Predictably, Luke asked, "A cat named Minnie?"

"It's spelled differently."

"Where's your car? I'll go get the cat." Mac offered.

"She hates men."

Luke watched her unease and commented cheerfully: "That's not surprising, somehow."

She gave him a cool look. "The day is beastly, the attendant gave me only a half hour to retrieve my car." She warmed to the drama of her words. "The heat is dreadful. It will be like an oven in my car, and Minny will die. I must go and get her out of the car. It's a death trap." She waited, trying to breathe normally. Would they buy it?

"It is a bad day," Mac said after a time.

"How can we take her outside?" Luke was practical.

"The fire stair?"

"And when we get her out to the car?"

Mac asked her, "Where are your keys?"

"There wasn't any need to lock it because I had to leave the windows open enough for her to have some air—however hot it was," she quickly amended.

With obvious reluctance, Luke decided, "So leave your purse here, and we'll go rescue the cat. If we see anyone, don't you say one word. Do you understand?"

"Of course." She gave him her best innocent look, but glanced away quickly. He wasn't a man one lied to, and her car keys were in the side pocket of her skirt.

Mac checked the hall, then stepped out and closed the door. After a minute he opened the door again, and beckoned with his whole hand to come on.

Luke took her arm and growled, "Not one word."

She nodded.

Since he was a leader and not a follower, he took his own look each way down the hall before he quickly pulled her along to the fire door Mac was holding open. They went through the door and down some raw utilitarian steps, along a narrow corridor and outside onto the parking lot. Georgia jerked her head around. Freedom, outside air, hot air, very hot pavement, not a soul around.

"Where...?" Her car wasn't anywhere in sight! "My cat!"

Luke explained: "Around the corner of the building." Then he said to Mac, "Watch for Herb or one of his goons."

"Hurry. I'll hold the door."

It wasn't an access door. There was no outside handle. Once closed, no one would be able to get inside through that door. So Mac would have to hold the door open. Only Luke would go with her to the car. She almost smiled.

His hand on her arm was more than a hold. In order to get away, she would have to leave her arm in his hand. How could she distract him? Make him loosen his grip and let go of her?

They went around the corner of the building and there was the front gate to freedom, and there next to the building was her pink car.

Luke stopped short. "Which is your car?" But he didn't sound as if he didn't know. Only one was parked next to the building. It was more as if he wanted a known reply. A confirmation.

"The pink—"

"Yes." And he pushed his lips together quite hard and his eyes squinted almost closed.

She could see the efficient gate attendant was aware of them. To be sure he was watching her and not Luke, she waved discreetly from her position somewhat behind Luke as he dragged her hurriedly along toward the pink car.

It was now! She screamed, *"Help! Call the police!"*

Luke stopped and looked at her in shocked irritation. The guard laughed!

"I'm being held prisoner!"

His back to the gatekeeper, Luke snarled a low sound, but the guard only laughed again and waved. Just because she'd told him the cat's name was Minny, the gatekeeper thought she was being funny? It didn't pay to joke with strange people. You might need them to take you seriously.

Over his shoulder, Luke grinned at the guard and with his free hand tousled Georgia's hair.

"I *mean* it!" she yelled. "Call the police! Help me!"

Luke turned her into his arms and his mouth came down on hers in the timeless way men have of silencing women instantly. Through the initial shock, erotica seeped into her bones. The kiss was devastating! It had been too long. Her body went mad. Her bones melted, her blood turned to fire, her mouth gave up. She was absolutely shameless. Slowly her free hand went up to the back of his head and she leaned her body into his as her mind departed for parts unknown.

When Luke lifted his mouth and looked down into her face, his eyes were smoldering fires of marvelous yellow colors, and she lay back on his arm waiting for more.

He said in a low, ruinous voice, "You said you wouldn't say a word."

With slow logic, she replied, "I said a bunch of words, not just one. You said 'a word,' but I said more than that." She almost smiled at him. Then her mind returned. She gasped. She blushed in a furious scarlet embarrassment and gave a token wiggle to escape. A feeble one. He released her! But he still held onto her arm. "You fight dirty," she accused.

He replied, "You do, too. Get the cat. You try yelling for help again and see what you get."

And she was tempted! What would he do? Her entire nervous system clamored for the risk. How shocking.

Two

While Georgia was deciding if she dared challenge Luke, Minny greeted them from inside the packed pink car. Georgia turned and stared at the stranger who was her cat. Luke opened the car door and Minny, her loyal and faithful companion, jumped easily onto his other arm and curled there!

"I thought she didn't like men." Luke gloated.

"Uh..." Obviously it was going to take a while to get over that one kiss. She'd be smart not to risk any more. She sent one more pitiful look at the attendant, who gave her another cheery wave. He would remember all this, in an interview on Cable News Network, after they found her dead body and that of her cat. No, the cat would take up residence with Luke, be perfectly happy and not even miss her.

As Luke hurried her around the corner and back along the stark side of the building, with Minny looking around from the shelter of his arm, Georgia mourned, "He didn't believe me."

"It's the pink car. How can anyone take someone seriously if she has a pink car?"

"I was going to have it painted."

"What color?" he asked with interest.

"I thought a dark green." He pulled her along several more steps before she asked, "After I'm dead, will you keep my car? File off the motor number and paint it?"

"Ms. Baines, nothing is going to happen to you. I've already promised you that. We just have to keep you and your busy little mind out of Herb's hands for a week or so."

"That's unlawful. False imprisonment. Being held against my will. It would go very bad for you."

"You'll have the best of care. I promise. Think of it as a vacation."

They'd reached Mac. "Hurry," he urged. "The hordes will be pouring out, it's almost five."

"Please!" Georgia tried once more.

"Don't worry. It'll be okay." Mac reassured her. "Get inside before anyone sees you."

"She asked Fred to call the cops." Luke had to tell that.

Mac laughed.

"It isn't funny! What if he was normal?" Luke hurried them down the hall.

"No one's normal who'd name a kid Albatross." Mac wasn't worried.

"Here's the albatross." Luke shook her arm a little. But her breast bounced, and he was distracted.

"Spunky McBaines." Mac glanced back at them.

"Georgia Baines." She was a little breathless from being hurried along that way—and from Luke's expression when he'd looked at her chest.

Mac exclaimed, "Sweet Georgia Brown."

"Baines," Georgia added.

Up the hidden stairs they went, and again Mac scouted the hall, waved them inside and they made it back to Luke's office. Luke let go of her arm, and she shook it to revive her circulation. He frowned a little. "Did I hurt you?"

"You paralyzed my arm. It'll be black and blue even if I recover the use of it."

He put Minny on his desk before he took Georgia's arm in his big hands and was careful in holding it. "I'm sorry. It's just that I've never captured a woman before and I'm not aware of some of the refinements. Be patient as we learn."

It was so logical. He wouldn't ever have to capture a woman in order to have one. He probably had to live very carefully and protect his address and phone number so that women didn't drive him crazy with their clamorings for his attention.

He released her arm with seeming reluctance, then he went into his bath/closet. He tore down the sides of a paper cup and filled the remainder with water for Minny.

The cat was charming. She lapped a little and waved her beautiful tail as if pleased. Minny didn't like water from a faucet. It had to be rainwater and she drank it only if it was spilled on the kitchen floor. The habit had been a big irritation. And here she was drinking chlorinated water from a paper cup for Luke. Georgia just said "Ah, Minny" in a knowing way. And Minny gave a snide little narrowing of her eyes. That only confirmed Georgia's opinion of the effect Luke had on females. Even cats.

They again sat around Luke's desk while Minny walked all over the room and its furnishings as she explored and commented.

"Why is your car packed full?" Luke asked suddenly.

"This is one of the questions you should have asked me at the beginning, before you both went absolutely around the bend and became paranoid and weird." She was very pleased with the logical sound, the maturity of her tone.

There was a little silence. "Would you have told us then?" Luke inquired politely.

She had neglected a reply. She lifted her nose. "I resigned my last position and am moving to Indianapolis to find a new one. I contacted a courier service to see if they needed anything brought here, and they did. Your letter. They paid my way here."

"You left Herb?"

Through her teeth she replied stridently, "I do not know any person named 'Herb.' "

"You realized he was using you and decided to escape."

"The only one I want to escape is you!"

"You still like Herb?" Luke appeared surprised.

Spacing the words carefully and enunciating them in a rather exaggerated manner, she repeated: "I do not know anyone named Herb."

"Where had you planned on staying tonight?"

"The Y."

"I wouldn't want anyone worried about you. Is there anyone who would worry if you don't contact them?"

Too quickly she replied eagerly, "My mother."

Both men looked at her suspiciously.

"I have to call her."

The men exchanged a glance before they studied Georgia. They were silent.

"She's a terrible worrywart. She'd have the FBI on your trail in no time. If you don't want to spend the rest of your lives behind bars..." She looked at Mac. "With Penny doing God only knows what with the people pouring out their troubles to her. You had better let me call my mother." She sat back satisfied.

"Pretty good," Luke complimented her.

"Not Academy Award." Mac shook his head.

"Well," Luke argued. "It was spur of the moment. You have to give points for that. Your mother abroad? Or is she deceased?"

Georgia sighed and admitted, "She's distracted. If you called her, she could have trouble placing my name, but in a couple of days she might remember me."

"Senile?"

"An actress. She's in a play right now and she really gets into her parts. She forgets the real world. You should have lived with her through *A Streetcar Named Desire*. Daddy almost left home."

"He's the one we have to call." Luke knew the answer.

"That's it," she agreed.

Mac said, "Don't let her call. You can't trust her an inch. You do it."

"I thought you'd do it." Luke was amused for some reason.

"Fathers have always had a strange aversion to me," Mac confessed. "Never knew why."

"Fathers are another race entirely," Luke explained as he sighed. "So. I'll call."

"What do you intend saying?" Georgia asked curiously.

"You have a code for him, too?"

"Of course not," she told Luke. "But you have to admit, if you were a father, and a strange man called up and said your daughter had arrived in Indianapolis safely, he might ask why she wasn't calling for herself."

"True." Mac rubbed his forehead. "This is getting complicated."

"I'd say you'd talked yourself hoarse, that your cat had escaped and you were chasing it, or I might say I had my hand over your mouth so I could get a word in edgewise. He'd believe that."

Georgia exclaimed in a disgusted sound.

"Do you want him to worry?" Luke's deep voice was gentle. "You will be all right. I've promised that, remember."

She didn't reply immediately but simply looked back at him before she said, "I have a headache and I'm hungry."

Minny easily hopped up onto the desk and weaved her lovely feline walk over to Luke to sniff his breath and then to curl down in front of his hands on his blotter.

"A headache?" Luke gave Georgia a look of concern. "I'd hate for you to take aspirin when you probably only need some food. It's almost five. Everyone who works here leaves immediately on the hour. It's an astonishing thing to watch. Then we'll go to my place and I'll feed you."

"What?"

"We could pick up burgers on the way," he offered.

"Sounds thrilling." She looked mournfully out the window at the lowering sky.

"How about Chinese?" Mac suggested. "I always get that for Penny when she looks out the window the way Georgia Brown is doing now."

"How?" Georgia asked curiously.

"Like you're friendless."

"Penny looks friendless?" Luke inquired.

"When she wants attention. Then I buy her Chinese."

"And that does the trick?"

"That and some hanky-panky." Mac grinned.

Luke, too, grinned, and then asked Georgia, "Chinese?"

She sat up straight and said, "Burgers will do very well."

And both men laughed.

Mac said quickly, "Hear that?"

There was a strange, almost frightening sound. An urgent, restless sound. "What is it?" It scared her a little. "The storm?"

"Come look." Luke went to the window. And she followed. An emergency? In the confusion, she could escape. She snatched up her purse and Minny and joined the two men at the window.

It was five o'clock on that Thursday evening. The sound was the employee exodus. How astonishing. They didn't run. They walked and talked, but the parking lot was emptied in four and a half minutes.

Everyone had left. Now Luke could take her to his place. And her captivity would begin. "It's time," said

Luke. "Let's go." He took Minny from Georgia and the little cat purred.

Mac refused to drive the pink car to Luke's place. "If I did, I'd see everyone I know, and I'd never live it down."

"Turn up your collar and wear your sweatband on your forehead." Luke gave him a bracing look. "You're of an age that you could be a residual hippie."

Quite casually Georgia suggested, "I'll drive it. Give me the address and I'll meet you there."

Mac agreed, "We could do that. We'd take the cat with us as hostage."

Minny lay in Luke's arms, very languorous and contented, while Georgia considered abandoning the cat. She couldn't. They'd been through too much together. She was silent as she waited for the men to face the fact one of them would have to drive the pink car.

"It's fortunate she has her own clothes." Mac's grin was wicked. "I can just see you buying her something to wear." He glanced at Georgia. "And you wearing it." Then he laughed.

"You're taking this in a very frivolous way." Georgia lifted her nose.

"Ex-NFL players are never frivolous," Mac replied. "At least, no one ever calls them that."

Georgia found herself smiling at him.

Mac grinned back, but by then she was looking at Luke. She could imagine what would happen to anyone rash enough to imply he was being less than manly. Then she looked at him more closely. Actually he could do just about anything and look perfectly comfortable doing it, even to driving a pink car.

"Mac, could you get us some groceries? I'll leave my car here." Luke had his gaze on Georgia. "I've got to get her fed. How's your head?"

"Splitting."

"Tension," Mac diagnosed. "Probably the first time she's ever been held captive. You were counting on her showing you how it's done, and she probably hasn't any idea at all."

"Completely mad, both of you!"

Luke chided, "I thought you weren't supposed to mention it."

"Neither of you could be unaware you're not working with a full deck. One of you must suspect it!"

"It's Luke." Mac confided instantly. "I'm his keeper. The family did this whole business setup so he could believe he's functioning—"

"You wouldn't believe how many times a quarterback gets sacked." Luke retaliated. "And with Mac, it was mostly on his head."

"A week of this?" Georgia threw out her arms.

"You'll adjust." Luke comforted her. "Anyone with a pink car and a cat named Minny is already halfway there."

"Is the gateman with the son named Albatross a relative?"

"Not close," Luke replied. "Fourth or fifth cousin on my father's side."

Mac chose then to say, "Well, I have to get home and see if Penny is looking pensively out the window, needing some Chinese. Good luck, you two. See you tomorrow, Luke."

"Follow us over to my place?"

"I was afraid of that. Now, how am I going to explain being late to Penny?"

"We'll think of something," Luke promised, and the two men began to escort Georgia down the same hidden stairs.

Helpfully she put in, "Tell Penny you're having an affair."

"My God! And you claim we're crazy? Do you know what she would do to me? I can't tell you on an empty stomach."

"Have you any cash on you?" Luke asked Mac.

Mac searched his pockets and came up with one dollar and thirty-seven cents.

Luke exclaimed, "Hell, I've only two bucks. How about you, Georgia?"

"I don't believe this. I'm supposed to feed you?"

"Now you couldn't eat in front of us, could you?" Luke was shocked. "Traveling, you have to be carrying some cash."

"Does the hamburger place honor credit cards?" She opened her purse.

"Not that I recall. I believe it's strictly cash and carry."

Mac slowly shook his head. "We just aren't set up to take a prisoner. We needed some warning so we could get organized."

"Give it up," Georgia suggested. "This whole thing is a fiasco. I don't know anything about the Molly Q. I don't know anyone named Herb. I'm no threat to you. Let me go. I'm tired. I'm getting cross. I want a bath. I'm hungry." She slumped a little.

They had exited the building and were walking to her car. Luke again promised: "We'll take good care of you."

Grittily she added, "After I've fed you."

"You don't have to feed me, too," Mac hastened to say. "I have to get home to Penny."

Luke eased Minny into the pink car, and on it's pink hood he wrote out a check and tore it from his book. "This is made out to you, Mac. Go to the grocery and get us the essentials for breakfast. Eggs, bacon, rolls, coffee—"

"Milk."

"Milk, butter... What else?" He looked at Georgia, politely sharing.

"Arsenic."

"No arsenic." He was sure. "If you will lend me enough to get the burgers, I can pay you back when Mac brings the change with the groceries."

"I don't believe this is happening."

Luke told Mac, "We'll see you as soon as you can make it."

"Call Penny for me and tell her I'm bringing home Chinese."

"Better not, she'll think you've been up to something."

"Not me," Mac denied a bit too elaborately, but making small circles with one hand he added, "just aided and abetted a capture of a strange female who is being held against her will, and who had to dish out the cash to feed herself. This has been an unusual day."

"Yes." Georgia could agree.

"Let's go." Luke started them off. Mac grinned and walked over to one of the few cars left on the lot. It was a station wagon. He gave a wave as he drove off.

Luke held out his hand for her car keys, and she dug them out of her pocket. Then she took a ten-dollar bill from her wallet and handed that to him, too. He thanked her gravely and stuffed it in his pocket. He took Georgia's arm in gentle fingers and walked with her to the passenger side of her car to help her inside and hand Minny to her.

He went back around the car and it took some struggle to fit his big body behind the wheel and try to push the seat back against the packed backseat in order to get a little room.

It had been unsettling enough to be in a room with Luke, but to be in the confined space afforded by her little pink car was almost overwhelming. She felt so— intimate. Did he feel it? He was so formidable. So masculine. So—close. She could put out her hand and lay it on his arm or his thigh. That strong muscled thigh was just under the smooth cloth of his pant leg. He was naked under those trousers.

Steady. He was her captor. He could well be as mad as she claimed. What was she doing in her very own car, driving God only knew where with this stranger?

"When we get to The Hamburger Haven, I'm going to park the car and take Minny with me to the carry-out window. If you say one word . . . *any words at all,* I will let Minny go. Do you understand?"

"Yes, sir."

"That's better. It's only for a week, and if you cooperate, this can be completely painless. As I said, think of it as a vacation."

"Do you have a maid?"

"A cleaning woman."

"Who cooks?"

"You don't?" He glanced briefly at her in surprise.

"Don't you?"

"I make a great can of tomato soup with cheese and crackers. I pour a mean bowl of Corn Flakes, and on occasion I make popcorn."

"A week?" she asked sourly. "This is going to be ghastly."

That offended him. "Attitude counts. It's how you approach things. You should look on this as an adventure. If you cooperate, we could have fun."

She slid a quick look at him, but he was watching the traffic. It could be that he didn't mean anything sexual about being cooperative. Her eyes went over his very nice face, his strong chest, his big, square, capable hands and down to that thigh again.

For all she knew, he might be gay. But the very thought made her bite her lip to keep from laughing and she had to look out her window until she could control her hilarity.

Luke might be a lot of things, but he was in no way indifferent to women. Not with the skilled, maddeningly marvelous way he could kiss. And he had been distracted when her breasts bounced. No, he wasn't indifferent.

She inquired, "How big is your place? Will your wife be there?"

"I'm not married any longer, and the place is an apartment. It's nice. However, there's only one bedroom."

Naturally. "Where will you sleep?" she asked sweetly.

"I'll think of something."

At the Hamburger Haven, while Luke and Minny went to the carryout window, Georgia sat in the pink car like a goof as she stared out at the low, dark clouds. She was holding a silent, intense discussion as to why she was just sitting there and not escaping. She had not reached a satisfactory answer when he returned.

He put the cat into the car window, got in and said, "They didn't have any deep-fried mice, but cats love french fries."

"Not Minny."

He just made a scoffing sound, dipped a french fry into his soda and offered it to Minny, who daintily nibbled it with all appearances of relishing hummingbird tongues. He couldn't just let it go, he had to say, "I know cats." And his yellow-brown glance lifted to hers as he smiled very knowingly about women, too. "I got you two cheeseburgers and a strawberry shake. And whatever french fries Minny won't eat."

Minny widened her green eyes and gave Georgia a very superior look.

Luke went on: "If you behave yourself and sit quietly, I'll let you eat your cheeseburgers here. Otherwise, we go home and you won't get out for at least a week. This is your last chance to be outside."

"I'm starving."

"Eat." He fished her two cheeseburgers out of the sack and put them on a napkin. "This is like a picnic." He seemed pleased.

"No ants."

Luke said around a mouthful of jumbo-burger with cheese, "We have a voracious beast, black with green eyes."

"Your hair is brown and your eyes yellow."

"My eyes are yellow?" He had to check the rearview mirror. "Naw. Brown." Then he looked at her sideways. "Do you think me beastly?"

"I have a broken arm to prove it."

His head snapped around and he frowned at her. He immediately put down the rest of the jumbo-burger and said, "Let me see!"

She lifted her broken wing.

He examined the already discernible marks left by his fingers and he was appalled. "I did hurt you!"

She was surprised he was so shocked. "It's not that bad."

"As soon as we get home, we'll give you some vitamin C, and we'll put some cold cloths on it. I'm sorry. I was afraid you'd get away."

They ate in silence. The sky was darker. The heat lessened and there was a slight breeze. Georgia lifted her face to it.

"Tired?"

"As Mac said, it's been an unusual day."

"Are you going to eat the other cheeseburger?" He inquired.

"No, you can have it."

"Well, if it's going to waste..."

His apartment was in a complex nestled in a woods. It was very attractive. Obviously expensive. The units were fieldstone, ivy-covered, with balconies. They were placed with calculation, so each unit was individual.

Mac was waiting for them, pacing on the sidewalk. The two men exchanged an amused male look. Mac said, "I got Minny some sand for her box. Some litter." He expected to be congratulated.

"We had some."

"I thought it was a stroke of genius."

Luke said, "It was. As soon as we get this stuff out of her car and upstairs, you can go home."

"Do you know, as I was loading the cart in the grocery store, I said to myself, 'Dollars to doughnuts, he'll ask me to haul all that stuff up those stairs.'"

"Any time you're ready."

"Give me the keys to open the trunk." Georgia slid that in very cleverly.

"I'll do that." But Luke was just being polite. That she might try to escape hadn't occurred to him. "How can one small girl and one tiny cat have so much junk?"

"No furniture." She commented.

Luke grinned. "I've been looking for a moving van."

They entered the apartment into the living room. It was long, with a bank of windows opening onto his balcony to the left. The kitchen was to the right with a dividing counter. There was an open door showing a bedroom. Another door to a bath, and the last door must be storage.

Georgia was left in the apartment, while the men took turns making trips up and down the stairs with her accumulated treasures, clothes, cat box and scratching post. Luke couldn't resist commenting on the scratching post. He asked Georgia, "Yours?" She didn't deign to reply.

When the last of her things had been brought upstairs, Georgia said to Mac, "In all good conscience, how can you leave me here all alone with this strange man?"

Instantly serious, Mac replied, "You will be perfectly all right."

If she had left it at that, they might have considered she was really afraid of Luke, and they would have reassured her, but then she said, "How do I know you aren't intending to sell me into white slavery? That he isn't an ax murderer? A sex maniac? You should stay here, too."

Patiently Mac explained, "Think of it like an office. It's no big deal. I would gladly stay, but if I don't get home tonight my wife would suspect something. She would never in this world think I was here as chaperon. She trusts me, but she doesn't trust other women. She thinks they all find me as fascinating as she does." He smiled smugly. "You should see the terror she chose as my secretary. And he's older, too."

Unfortunately Georgia laughed, and the two men relaxed and didn't take her seriously after that. Trying again not to be left alone with that dangerously attractive man, she pleaded with Mac, "Doesn't it bother you to just leave me here with him?"

"Him? Naw. I trust him. Oh, you mean—him male, you female? You don't have a thing to worry about. Luke's thirty-five. He was some jock in his day, but he's burned out. Women don't interest him any more."

And Luke had the gall to duplicate the wickedly innocent look of David Lee Roth.

While Georgia could only be astonished, Mac rubbed his face with both hands, as if in grief. "Maybe some day a kind woman will take him in hand and bring him back."

Luke turned away and bowed his own face in his hands . . . and his shoulders shook.

Georgia coughed. "So," she said in a steadied voice, "you don't like women?"

Luke turned back to her. "Women? Of course, I do. But only as friends. Good friends." And the David Lee Roth look was back.

There was a silence. Then Mac said cheerfully, "I'm on my way. I'll come around about ten tomorrow and check things out. Mind now, Sweet Georgia Brown, leave him alone. It would be futile."

She was still inhaling for her reply after the door closed.

It was awkward being just the two of them, there in that silent apartment. It was a nice place, but bland. She moved, looking around, trying to appear casual. He lifted the sacks of groceries and carried them into his small kitchen.

She glanced at her things stacked on one side of the forgettable living room. What was she doing in this situation? How incredible!

Three

———

Luke efficiently put away the foodstuffs. Then he took the kitchen phone, unplugged its jack, carried it over and opened the storage door, but it was a second bedroom. Georgia watched. He'd said one bedroom. So there was another.

However, the room was furnished as an office. There was a computer with its printer on a table against one wall, a desk with its chair's back to the wide window, there was a couch, and bookshelves ran along one wall. The surfaces weren't at all tidy. Papers were stacked, books were lying helter-skelter, and the room spoke of a man too involved, too rushed. He was a workaholic?

Luke put the kitchen phone in a desk drawer. Then he came to the door of the room and said with gentle seriousness, "Georgia, I think you should call your folks. I have to ask that you don't betray us. You must take my word that no harm will come to you, and that I am being honest with you when I tell you how important this is to our company. If Herb knew you'd seen the plans for the Molly Q, he would go to any ends to find them out—from you. I don't want your parents to worry. If I let you call, will you just tell them you are only temporarily settled? You can give them this number as a place to contact you."

She considered how earnest he was. He had to trust her to allow her the phone call. She watched him, studying him, thinking about him. Minny trusted him. The only man Minny trusted. But look at the man! Think of his gentle hands on that cat. How he spoiled her. Dipping the french fries in his soda, ruining the drink because salt wasn't good for little cats.

And his friendship with Mac. Either could ask the other anything. Their friendship must go back to a time before they worked together. How easy they were with their exchange of humor. Luke would have many men friends like Mac. Men would like him.

So would women.

"Promise you'll just say you're safe. And Georgia, you are safe. Just say you've arrived and you'll be in touch. Give them this number. All right?"

He had such a nice face. His yellow eyes were so honest. He was a little tired. He said she was the first woman he'd ever captured. She smiled a little, and he smiled back.

"Okay?"

She nodded. It was as if she'd cast the dice in his favor. As if she'd capitulated. As if she had given up her rights. As if she'd put her hands out to his fire because he had told her it wouldn't harm her.

"What's the number?"

She automatically replied, and he watched her lips say the numbers.

Luke punched the code, and reached out to draw her next to him as he put the phone between them. It began to ring.

Luke had a wonderful smell to him, his own skin's fragrance. She was very close to him. She could hear him breathe. How alive he was. How vital.

It rang again.

Luke had a good beard. He hadn't shaved since morning, and if she put her hand on his cheek she would feel the prickles.

With the third ring, he turned his head a little and looked down at her. He gazed into her eyes and then glanced at her mouth.

She licked her upper lip. It was only a quick, nervous lick. It wasn't a slow sensuous, flirting one. But her tongue had gone ahead and done that, and she blushed.

The fourth ring. Weren't they home? No one? How embarrassing. She'd tell him they were at the FBI filling out a report.

Five rings. She looked at his hand so easily holding the mouthpiece end of the phone. How masculine. Square, blunt fingers, hard-looking. So gentle on that wickedly smug cat. So gentle on her wounded arm.

Six? She sighed and looked up at him as his gaze dropped down to her chest. She too looked down to the crumpled orange that covered it, and she blushed again as she saw that her heart was thudding so hard the material trembled.

"You're okay. It's all right." His voice was deep and comforting. He thought she was afraid? Here she was restraining herself from touching his raspy beard, touching his lower lip, and—

Seven.

"Everyone always thinks someone else will answer," she explained as she looked up into his eyes. He smiled a little and nodded.

Good God, eight! She could feel the heat of his body and it was exciting hers. She really ought to step away a little—

The receiver lifted and a male voice rasped, "Browns'."

"Daddy?"

"Depends on who you are." His rough voice was droll.

"It's me."

"Well, of course! You're my second oldest, if I remember correctly."

"Uh..." She sent a quick look up at Luke. He tensed a little. She said, "I'm here."

"That's interesting to hear."

"I have a number you can reach me."

"*Where* I can reach you?"

"Yeah." She read the number off the card on the phone.

"Are you all right, Sweet Georgia?"

She exchanged another glance with Luke. "Yes." It was softly said.

"Get in touch with the Gradys right away," his rasping voice advised. "Are you sure you don't want to stay with them?"

"I'll...see."

"Take care, baby. Keep in touch."

"Bye, Daddy."

Luke hung up the phone and never took his stare from her. He leaned to kiss her mouth, but Georgia stepped away.

She couldn't allow another of his kisses. One had boggled her, and she was his captive. She hadn't alerted her father, but he had the phone number. They could trace her if they needed to, if she vanished from the face of the earth. Her eyes were very vulnerable.

Luke watched her, then he asked, "Brown? Sweet Georgia Brown, the way Mac said?"

"Daddy loves the song. He said I didn't have any options. He named me before I was born. Probably the night I was conceived. He knew I'd be a girl and I'd be named Georgia."

Cautiously he questioned, "Baines?" as he raised his brows just a little.

"I was widowed two years ago."

He lifted his hand and smoothed the hair back from her face, not saying anything. How could he possibly say he was sorry? But he pitied the dead man who had lost her.

He said, "Go take a good, deep bath. Do you have any oils or bubbles or something you like? I have soap. That's all. I'll change the sheets."

"I can do that."

"Vitamin C. For your bruises. I feel awful that I hurt your arm, but I was afraid you'd bolt." His voice was low and a little reedy.

Distant thunder rumbled, and he ran a soothing hand down her back to her waist. Then he became brisk, straightened, unplugged that phone jack and proceeded to lock both phones in the bottom drawer. "That's just in case you sleepwalk." He grinned at her.

* * *

It seemed vulnerable to be taking a deep bath in a strange man's apartment. What if he broke down the door to get to her? She cupped her hands and scooped up the warm water to let it flow down her arms. She considered how she would look astonished and rise like Venus from her half shell to stand back modestly—inadequately covering herself with her hands.

There were the towels. She could wrap her entire body, hands and feet in the towels. She discarded that idea and went back to considering him advancing toward her from the shattered bathroom door, his yellow eyes burning with passionate fires, unable to stop himself.

If he was so overwhelmingly attracted, he had been alone with her since Mac left. There was no need to break down the bathroom door. He could just wait until she unlocked it and opened the door. Then—

There was an electrifying tap on the door and Luke called, "Are you all right? You need to come on out of there."

She sat up straight with the sound of his knock, and she felt her heart thudding in excitement. What did he have in mind?

"Georgia!"

It was happening! He was going to break down the door! She'd be helpless. He would scoop her up and carry her up the stairs— No stairs. He would take her in on those fresh sheets and—

"Georgia! You're not slitting your wrists or anything, are you?"

It was only worry. Not sex. "I'm fine."

"You make me nervous, taking so long. Come on out and tell me what to put away."

"Put away?" Where? His things filled everything. There wasn't any room to put anything of hers away.

But she quickly finished bathing, dried and put on blue-and-green two-inch-wide vertical-striped pajamas. She frowned because they were sleeveless and only to her mid thigh. Did they seem . . . inviting?

She was more covered than if she was wearing a bikini. And the thought of wearing her purple bikini for him flooded her with sensations. She would drive him wild, but she'd be casual about it. "This old thing?" she'd say disparagingly.

"Georgia!"

"All right! I'm coming!" And she blushed as she arranged her sleek brown mane into casual disarray. Why, Georgia!

She opened the door of the bathroom and stood a minute, allowing him to see her, to look at her. He was standing at the southwest window, looking outside, holding Minny, as the drapes blew out in the mounting wind. The storm was making the sky black too early and the thunder was closer.

"I opened up the apartment. Smell the air!"

The August night was cool and the rain smell was deliciously fresh. There was something exciting, exhilarating about storms, and Georgia wasn't afraid of them. They made Minny nervous. The cat curled in Luke's arms and blinked contentedly at Georgia. Minny was a fraud.

Georgia stood at the window near Luke. She found the man more exciting than the storm. She must be especially vulnerable for some reason. Was it the age-old helplessness of the captive maiden and the handsome captor? Surely not. There must be another reason.

She should do something to distract herself. She looked around. In the bedroom was a sturdy hanging rack. And there was an additional chest of drawers.

"Where did you get those?" she asked Luke.

"I called the complex office. Sometimes they have extras. I've rented those for your stay. You'll be more comfortable with your things sorted."

It seemed so permanent to put things away, to settle in. That was a very dangerous thing for an attractive bachelor to do with a strange woman. How reckless of him! He might have a hard time getting rid of any other woman.

She went to the pile of clothes that had been suspended on hangers from a bar in the backseat of her car, and began to carry the first bunch into the bedroom.

Luke put the cat down and helped.

Her watercolors and paintings were stacked to one side in a corner of the living room. The needlepoint pillows were jewels of design and color. She pitched them onto his mud-colored sofa, and they landed like butterflies on dirt to glow there.

Her boxes of books and art equipment were put to one side, and the crocheted bedspread was laid on the great king-size bed. The spread would be inadequate for that expanse.

It was very strange to put her intimate things into a chest of drawers in a strange man's bedroom. It was as if she had agreed to her captivity.

The storm was closer. The sound of it was intrusive. Luke had to close windows against the beginning, wind-driven rain which splattered against the glass and swept on past. Georgia could feel the trembling of the storm through her feet as the thunder shook the building.

The trees bent and turned their leaves to be washed clean. And Minny sat in Luke's arms, her eyes enormous as she jerked her head around, watching.

How clever of the cat to be nervous of storms and need Luke's care. Could a grown twenty-eight-year-old self-supporting woman be jealous of a cat? Apparently.

It became much darker. Luke didn't put the lights on, nor did he close the drapes against the storm. He sat down on the sofa, holding the cat, and he patted the place next to him, inviting Georgia to sit, too. She hesitated, but the temptation was too great and she eased down near him.

"It's a great show," he commented. "Have you ever been out on a field or a prairie and watched one?"

"On the shore at Myrtle Beach."

"Yes. I was on a ship in the middle of the Atlantic and saw one. It makes a believer of you."

"Me and you, God?"

"Exactly."

The tumult went on, and the cat was restless. Georgia became sleepy and said she thought she'd just go on to bed.

"I did get a portable bed that's in the study. It sags in the middle. But there is that great bed in the other room, and you're really a very small girl. You don't take up much room at all, and you won't be using up nearly half of that big bed, and even with Minny taking up the middle, there'd still be room enough for me."

"Uh—"

"It's called bundling." He ignored her attempt to interrupt. "A good old American custom. We'll have Minny down the middle as the bundling board, and we'll both be comfortable. If the storm gets worse, you'll be able to hold my hand without getting out of bed."

"I'm not afraid of storms."

"How do you know I was talking about you? I might very well be terrified of storms."

"You're comforting Minny."

"No, no, no. She is comforting me!"

"Balderdash."

"Not bundling is un-American."

"You get the cot."

"How about trading? Every other night?"

"No." But the sound was soft, for her mind was swamped at the image of sharing a bed with this man. It had been too long.

"I can't believe you're this hard-hearted. You have such—" He raised up, interrupting his coaxing. "Shh!"

She waited, listening. A tornado? Finally she whispered, "What is it?"

Minny wasn't alarmed. She wasn't listening, so it wasn't a mouse or anything awful. Georgia took a breath to speak.

"Shh." He took her hand and held her still. Then he gave her Minny, and said against her ear, "I'll go look. Don't move. Understand?"

She nodded. She felt bug-eyed in the dark. What was it? He moved without a sound in the storm's fury. He disappeared like a shadow. She was impressed. He was there—then he was gone. She was alone. What was the matter?

Her ears strained and her head turned as she sought clues. Nothing in the apartment moved. All she could think of was the classic, "It was a dark and stormy night..." It was dark and stormy, and there was something wrong?

When he returned, it was so quickly, soundlessly done that she squeaked with alarm. Minny had moved her head, Georgia looked down at the cat and Luke was back beside her. On her lap, Minny began to purr.

He lied quietly, "I'm not sure. But it could be someone was nosing around. We might have to move you to another place to keep you safe from Herb."

"I really have no idea who Herb is, and I have never had any dealings with someone by that name. I don't know him. I'm not a corporate pirate, nor do I know anyone who is." She was very earnest.

He patted her shoulder. "I'll check with security. It could be nothing, but it's better to be safe. Herb would do anything to get his hands on you. You must understand that. I got rid of your car."

That took a minute to sink in before she gasped, "What?"

"Your car is an eye-catcher. You have to admit that. I couldn't have it down on the street screaming for attention. So I got rid of it."

She immediately pictured her little car falling off a cliff into a boiling river, never to be seen again. There weren't any cliffs around. There was the quarry down by Bloomington... "What did you do with it?" she asked in dread.

"Sent it to storage. It's safe and sound. Just out of sight."

"Oh." So it was safe, but with her car unavailable a great chunk of opportunity to escape was eliminated.

By then the rain was simply rain. The wind had moderated, the lightning and its resulting thunder were gentled by distance as the storm swept on to the northeast. Georgia was tired. Rather awkwardly she said, "Well, good night." Did one observe the amenities with captors? What did Emily Post say about that?

He rose politely and followed her toward the bedroom door. She tensed. Did he intend going to bed, too? Did he intend sleeping with her, after all? What would he do? Was he...would he? She turned and faced him. "Uh." What could she say?

"Sleep well." His voice was deeply masculine and touched the words softly.

Georgia would be there alone with Luke. She shivered and put her arms around herself.

He noted the movement. "Don't be scared. You'll be safe. I'll take good care of you." Then he added almost as if it was an afterthought: "Herb can't get into the apartment."

She looked at him blankly. She wasn't afraid of Herb. She was only afraid of her own reaction to Luke. She didn't know any Herb. He might be some threat, but she felt completely protected with Luke. He was invincible.

"Good night, Sweet Georgia Brown." He smiled down at her and one of his big, blunt fingers slid a strand of her tumbled hair back from her forehead. It was very like a caress.

Her lips parted and she said, "Yes." Since she wasn't paying any attention, the word sounded perfectly logical to her.

She picked up Minny, went into the bedroom and slowly closed the door. She walked over to the big bed and dropped the little cat on the end of it. The bed was too big for one person.

Thoughtfully she removed the hidden hairpins which had held the casual disarray she'd deliberately created—and which should have embarrassed her. She brushed her hair as she strolled aimlessly around the room, not paying any particular attention to either directing her steps or to the brushing.

Minny sat on the bed and watched her with quickly dwindling interest before she looked around the room. She hopped down and investigated the clothes rack more minutely, then leaped up on the new chest and walked around. Finally she dropped down to the floor, went over to the door and sat there. She looked at Georgia, gave an encouraging mew and waited.

Georgia was at the window looking out at the rain, or her gaze was aimed in that direction. The complex had well-placed, discreet lighting, and the shimmer of the drops was discernible. The outside world was uninvitingly wet.

Minny gave another mew, and when Georgia didn't respond quickly enough, the cat stretched her little body up, wrapped her forepaws around the doorknob and turned it as she walked her back feet enough so that the door opened minutely. Then she dropped down on all fours, pushed her nose into the opening and left the room. She had never learned to close doors.

Still in her bemusement, Georgia folded and lifted her crocheted bedspread onto a chair, pulled back the spread and opened the welcoming envelope of bed-clothes to crawl inside.

She was tired. She lay thinking over her incredible day. Who would ever believe it? She'd gotten up that morning, wiped away the last trace of herself as she vacated her apartment near Cleveland, gone to a café for breakfast, innocently collected The Envelope and driven to her destiny. Astonishing. Here she was in Luke Montana's apartment, lying in his bed.

How clever of him to rent that cot, the rack for her clothes and the chest of drawers. Very efficient.

If he hadn't had a place to sleep and had tried to fit his big body on that living-room sofa, how long would it be before she would say, "I'll take the sofa"? Would she be such a wimp as to do that? Probably.

It's what her mother, Felicia, would do for her dad. For all Felicia's airy life-style, she really stroked her husband. "This is the best piece, and it's your fa-ther's," she'd tell the children. There was no discern-ible difference in the pieces, but she had labeled his piece the best.

Felicia would say, "Sit here, darling, it's more comfortable." She'd smile at him and pat a pillow. She would look at her husband, her eyes big and her small mouth serious, as she'd say, "I need you. Without you, I'd be lonely."

The kids used to laugh at their mother for saying that because there were always so many of them.

Georgia sighed and spread her arms and legs out on the big bed and couldn't reach any of the edges. It was too big for one person, one woman, one woman alone.

She heard the squeak and thump as Luke got onto the cot. It groaned and complained as he tried to get comfortable.

Portable beds were awful, convenient torture racks. They always sagged in the middle. If they were called hammocks, it would be more honest. Calling them beds made the victim assume he could sleep on his side or even try to sleep on his stomach. It never worked. Poor Luke.

Now, why should she pity him? Look where she was because of him! Him and his paranoid imaginings about some spook named Herb and a blueprint called the Molly Q.

Molly Q. What a name for a project! Men are so interesting. Look at their words. Calling a project the Molly Q. It was like the romantic terminology for corporate takeovers she'd read about in *Time*: The Golden Parachute, White Knight, Pac-Man Defense, Scorched Earth, Shark Repellent and the Poison Pill.

Basically, men were warriors. All of life was a game plan to them. Competition. How fascinating men are. Just look at Luke and Mac. They thought Herb was after the Molly Q, and that Georgia was a lamb for a tiger. No woman would be so paranoid.

Here she was, lying in a strange bed, a corporate captive in a perfectly ridiculous affair of male imagination. Men playing games of King of the Mountain. Big games. Serious games that affected lives and money. Her life.

How did Luke feel about having her there and taking the responsibility for holding her there a week? Disrupting her life. What if she'd had a job? Or what if she had a family? Would he still have so ruthlessly redirected her life? He hadn't inquired if it was convenient for her to take this…vacation, as he called it.

How to explain such strange behavior in an apparently stable man? Well…he'd walked into the conference room, seen her and fallen madly in love? He'd instantly concocted this entire plot to have her at his fingertips, to court her, possess her and sate his mad lust for her gorgeous body? Yeah. Sure. She smiled into the night over such a silly idea.

But wasn't he the most beautiful man she'd ever seen! He moved with such easy male grace, his big, hard hands were so masculine.

Now, just a minute here, she said to herself with some irritation, just back off and quit being such a nerd. Here you are, this man has you captive against your will, and you think he's gorgeous and moves like a god…and you regret taking his bed! Dumb.

It just didn't pay to get too friendly with an unlawful captor. If he would hold a woman captive, he might well have other flaws. She should stay aloof from him. If she acted like a wimpy victim, she would be treated like one.

She was a full-grown woman. She had rights. She must assert herself. It was as her grandmother had always told them, "You're the captain of your ship and the master of your soul, by the Lord Harry."

Who was Lord Harry? Henry VIII? Her grandmother had seemed old enough to have known Henry well. He'd certainly run things his own bloody way, chopping off heads. If you did do things your way, it wasn't decent to interfere with other people's rights.

Like Luke Montana was interfering with the life of Georgia Brown Baines. How dare he do this to her? Where was her backbone? Just because he was so wondrous to see, and so positive that he had every right to do as he chose, didn't mean she should meekly go along with him and allow all this!

There she was in his bed. Imagine that! Where was he?

She listened. All was still. It was strange. There seemed to be a life to the apartment that was its own. The place seemed alive. It seemed to breathe.

It was Luke's passionate breathing. He was waiting for her to fall asleep, and then he would sneak in here and crawl naked into her bed. He would insinuate himself over by her, his breathing roughened and he would slowly, sneakily take her into his arms. Then he would very carefully touch his mouth to hers.

While she was being surprised about that, he would undo her green-and-blue striped cotton pajamas and push them aside. And he would have to straighten up enough to admire her body lying there like a feast before him.

Georgia could feel her cheeks heat in embarrassment over her silly thoughts. But . . . would he?

The cot creaked in the next room. She tensed. He was getting up! He was starting for her! She was helpless! Then she saw the door was open!

Minny. Minny was gone. She'd opened the door and left. Deserted by her own cat. And there she was in Luke's bed and he was easing off the cot to sneak in and have his wicked way with her.

And he snored.

He was asleep. He didn't want his wicked way with her. He was tired and asleep on that diabolical portable bed. He must be exhausted, to sleep under these circumstances. How did he know she wouldn't attack him?

Well. If she was going to escape, now was the golden opportunity. He was asleep. She needed only to get out of bed, open the apartment door and—leave. Now.

It . . . was . . . a comfortable bed. Cozy in the rainy night. She rolled over, not trying to be quiet, and she felt a little irritated that she ought to do something right now about this mess she was in. She was tired.

He was asleep. Now was the time.

She scowled, threw back the covers and sat on the edge of the bed like a reluctant lump. Her car was unavailable. All her worldly possessions were in this apartment. She would have to walk somewhere on this dark and rainy night, ask someone to help her *and* convince them she wasn't some kind of nut walking around in the rain in blue-and-green striped cotton pajamas, carrying a wet, black cat who would be in something of a temper.

But Luke was asleep. She was not a victim. She was Captain of her Soul and all that stuff. She should, in all good conscience and in the American way, get off that bed and get away. It was her duty.

She heaved up off the bed and fished around on the dark floor for her shoes. She put them on slowly, listening to Luke, who was a rotten guard if he couldn't hear his own prisoner sigh and bump into things. He still snored. Dead to the world. Just exactly as if he had a clear conscience.

She gave a farewell look at her things, neatly stored in her captor's bedroom, opened the door farther and went out into the living room.

Luke had a wonderful snore. It was a soft, comforting type, which said the warrior wasn't worried, everything was under his control. It was even nicer than her daddy's. Her dad's snore had made all the kids feel secure. Luke's snore was like that.

She was going to take Minny and leave the security of Luke's snore and go out into the dark and stormy night and face... what?

She stood in the living room, uncertain. Where was Minny? Georgia couldn't help the noise she made as she looked for the cat. Minny was nowhere around! Where was Minny? Where had she gone? Had the cat escaped? Like Lassie? Gone for help?

The door to Luke's study was only slightly open. About Minny wide. Could Minny, her very own cat, be fraternizing with the enemy?

Georgia pushed the door open Georgia-wide, and there on Luke's chest, blinking lazy eyes and looking smug, curled Minny. She, who didn't like men, was purring.

Georgia wondered if she should risk retrieving her cat, or if she should abandon the wanton. She whispered, "Come here." Then, ignored, she ground out, "Minny!"

Sleeping the conscienceless sleep of the self-deluded, Luke bubbled on. Georgia stood there, comforted by his snore, contemplating the rain, the contented cat and the choice she had.

She went back to the other bedroom. Having closed the door, she sat on the edge of Luke's bed, removed her shoes and pulled the sheet and summer quilt over her. She plumped the goose-down pillow, as her guilt nudged one final time. She thought to hell with it, and she went to sleep.

Georgia didn't waken until just before ten. She stretched and yawned and felt great. She smiled,

opened her eyes and realized where she was and why.
She sighed, turned over and considered her attitude.
If the country depended on her, it was due a disap-
pointment. A little rain had stopped her from escaping. How embarrassing.

She deliberately made some noise. The door was
Minny-open and Luke would have to know she was
awake. It was very silent in the rest of the apartment.
He would have to hear her.

She yawned again, making some sound with it, and
allowed small, contented noises as she stretched. She
did that as if she wasn't awake enough to recall that
she was a captive.

Minny came through the door and mewed a greeting. Georgia eyed the faithless cat and shook her head
in censure.

Minny blinked slowly and sat down by the door.

Four

___

As she rose from the bed, Georgia inquired, "Well, Minny, I suppose you've had breakfast?" The Browns always spoke to their pets as if they could understand, because they probably could.

Minny lifted one paw and gave it a couple of licks in reply. She had eaten.

"More french fries?"

Minny turned her head away enduringly.

Georgia tapped on the connecting door to the bath, and receiving no reply, opened it cautiously as if the Creature from the Black Lagoon might be lolling in the tub. It wasn't there and neither was Luke.

She showered, put on a soft, dark green terry jogging suit and twisted her freshly washed hair into a soft swirl on the back of her head. She put loops in her ears and brushed her eyelashes with enough color to be seen. Then, since she was a prisoner, she added just a bit of white powder to her cheeks, so that she wouldn't look too healthy.

She went back into the bedroom and put her things away. Then she opened the door of her room—Luke's room—and inadvertently touched a string which caused a loud clang! She yelped. And the door of the second bedroom burst open to reveal Luke.

He looked around quickly as if he expected to see the mysterious Herb with her over his shoulder. Since Herb wasn't there, only she, he grinned and said, "Good morning, sleepyhead."

Behind him, also very alert, was Mac. He teased her late rising. "We figured, when you said you were going to retire, you just meant for the night! We didn't know you meant we wouldn't see you for the whole week. Didn't you get hungry?"

Georgia gave him a patient look, then her eyes followed the Rube Goldberg alarm system before she asked, "You expected me to escape?"

The two men exchanged a glance before Luke said, "Or that Herb would make a try for you."

She scoffed.

Luke told her, "I'll make some waffles."

Mac amended. "He doesn't make them, they're frozen. You just put them in the toaster."

She went into the kitchen, and the two men and the little cat trailed along. She opened the refrigerator and looked inside. She contemplated milk, butter, eggs, bacon and several shelves of beer.

The men and cat sat and watched her as she fixed herself bacon and eggs, then they breathed the aroma and smacked their lips, and she ended up making enough for them all.

They did wait until she was seated at the table before they began to eat, and Mac did make the toast. She told Mac, "He got rid of my car."

"Of course," Mac agreed.

"Of course?" She was indignant.

"Well, you're not going anywhere. And it isn't as if it wouldn't be noticeable out on the street. Why did you have it pink?"

"I worked for a florist. On occasion, I would deliver unscheduled bouquets. It seemed more...festive to have the car...different."

Both men made small sounds that acknowledged the speech but didn't commit them to having to give an opinion. However, in doing that, they had given an opinion.

Luke's eyes smiled at her. "How'd you sleep?"

"Quite well," she told him stiffly. "And you?" She raised her eyebrows just a tad.

He complained. "I felt as if a car had a wheel resting on my chest with its motor running. It was your man-hating cat." His eyes invited her to laugh with him over Minny's liking him.

She didn't allow herself to accept that, but she had to drop her gaze to her plate to hide it. She covered her move by commenting to the cat, "Gaining a little weight with french fries for supper?" Minny didn't even bother to glance at her over that comment. So Georgia asked Luke, "Did Minny have breakfast?"

"Oh, yes." Luke was giving the cat a lick of egg yolk from his finger, and she was daintily touching his finger with her tiny tongue.

Georgia watched that and again found she was envious of the cat. Not, she assured herself, that she wanted to lick egg yolk from Luke's finger...Yes, she did. If she got down on the floor, would he offer her some? And she smiled a little over the mental picture of her down, shoving the cat aside, and—

Luke said, "She had a little bacon, a part of a waffle, some canned cat food, a bit of creamed coffee and an antacid."

Georgia was shocked.

Luke added blandly: "She didn't want any sugar in her coffee."

"You're going to kill her. French fries, coffee, bacon—"

Mac put in chewingly: "All cats like coffee."

Georgia ignored cat preferences. "What did your wife have for dinner last night?"

"I was just a tad late getting there. Too late to go to the deli. So I got out of the car and leaned pensively on it and looked into the distance. If you recall, it was getting ready to storm. The wind was blowing what hair I have left, I let my shoulders slump and I stood there for a while.

"Pretty soon Penny came out and put her hand on my shoulder and said, 'Mac?' in her special voice. I sighed a very long sigh and said, 'It's *really* a jungle out there. You have no idea the cost in stress.'"

"You didn't!" Georgia was indignant.

"Oh, yes. Women can't always have things their way."

"How did it work?" Luke was curious.

"Fantastic. She wanted me to quit, but—"

"*Quit!*" Luke roared.

"Be calm." Mac pacifyingly raised both hands and made his face benign. "I agreed—"

"You can't!"

"Luke, be quiet. You're ruining my story!"

"Okay, so you said you'd quit me."

"I only said it, Luke, I didn't actually *sign* anything. You tend to be hysterical."

Georgia asked, "What happened?"

"I told her I would quit Montana and get an easier job. That I'd always liked lobsters, and I thought I'd become a lobster fisherman. Man against the sea. She was very brave about it. I was impressed. We got into a long discussion of what we want out of life and how we look at things. It was great. To think it started out with me trying to weasel out of being late getting home, and we had the best discussion in all our married life. I won't use the 'jungle out there' again soon, but it's nice to know how much she loves me. That I'm important to her."

Georgia smiled at him.

"And how about you children? Did you get along all right?" And Mac's grin was wicked.

Luke said dangerously, "There's no call for your stupidity, so cut it out."

Mac raised his eyebrows and grinned. "Oh-ho!"

"Mac," Luke warned.

"Yes, sir. Yes, sir. Very good, sir." He turned to Georgia. "Have I told you yet that I was under Luke in 'Nam? We were both eighteen, and he was a corporal. He got me home."

It was difficult to feel properly hostile to captors who treated one in this casual social manner. It was better than blindfolds and tied wrists, but it did make it difficult to be aloof and indignant.

So she said coolly, "I'm going to sue you and your company for one hundred thousand dollars unless you let me go." She sat back and waited for their shocked protest—and her release.

Luke instantly replied, "If we can keep the lid on the Molly Q for just ten days, we'll *give* you the hundred thou."

Georgia blinked at him in a very Minny-like way. She said, "Uh..." and couldn't think of anything for a minute. She hadn't expected that kind of calm reaction. She should have said ten million. It was just as ridiculous. Why not think big?

Very businesslike, Luke rose from the table as he said, "I'll be back in about an hour. It might take two."

Georgia stared at him.

"I'll be back." He then said it to her.

She didn't reply, but just looked at him as he winked at her and smiled slightly before he left.

"Where's he going?" Her eyes went to Mac who was watching her intently.

"Errands."

In the maxi-minutes of the endless time that followed, she missed Luke. How silly. She'd not even known him for a whole day. But he left on errands, and she missed him?

It was probably just that with him gone she couldn't be released. That was it. She needed him there to convince him to let her go.

She automatically cleaned up the kitchen. Then she joined Mac in the living room to watch the rest of Phil Donahue on TV.

She checked her watch now and then. She'd get up restlessly and walk around. She needed some exercise. "Could we go for a walk?" She distracted Mac from a soap opera and had to repeat the question.

His eyes never leaving the TV screen, he replied, "No. If I lost you, I'd never hear the last of it."

"I just need some exercise."

"Scrub the kitchen floor."

She went back to pacing. But when Luke returned, she sat down and was quiet. And Mac pushed his lower lip up and studied her as Luke gave him instructions to take back to the office.

When Mac left, he said loudly enough for Georgia to hear, "Keep track of her expenses. It's a straight hundred thou. No frills. She pays her own way."

Luke laughed, but Georgia yelled back, "I can handle daily expenses for an overall recovery of a hundred *thou.*"

Mac waved to indicate he'd heard and went off. They were again . . . alone.

Luke had brought groceries. He sorted them out and put them away before he went into his study to sit at his desk. The phone rang and he had to unlock the bottom drawer to pull out the phone. He talked, leaning back in his big swivel chair, gesturing lazily, absently ruffling his hair. It rang again, now and then, but not too much. Obviously he delegated some authority and didn't have to be endlessly consulted. But he was busy.

She dragged a string along the floor for Minny to stalk, watched out the windows at the rain, went over the TV guide and watched a *National Geographic* and a *Nova.* An exciting day. With Luke watching her through his door, it was exciting.

They were still a bit awkward at the late lunch. She shouldn't have chatted with him, but if she talked to him she had the excuse to look at him.

They had deli sandwiches and snacks. With lunch over, he said, "I enjoyed your company." And he smiled at her very nicely before he went back to work in his study. But she would glance up at him, and he'd look up and smile at her.

With another day past, she again slept in his bed, listening to the portable bed creak and groan with his restless attempts to find a comfortable position.

The next day, he cooked for them quite cheerfully. He was really pretty good. Besides tomato soup, he cooked steaks. Actually he only seared them. She had to have hers a little "browner."

And they talked. Each meal was easier. Their exchange became quick and humorous with their tales of childhood and school. They spoke of people they knew or had known, and they shared stories about their families. They began to know each other.

He had to check her bruised arm. His fingerprints on her white skin were now a gorgeous slate blue color. He used the opportunity to smooth his big hand gently along her arm, then he kissed it. Each spot. He lifted his head to be sure he'd kissed them all. It was very erotic to her.

He finally had to ask about her husband. He really didn't want to talk about a man who had slept with her, but he felt he had to know. "You said you're a widow?"

"Two years."

"What happened?"

"He was hit by a car." Her voice was soft. Georgia went on, "He was a man who never lifted his voice. He was a troubadour and should have had a patron so that he could have spent his time composing his songs...dreaming. And he must have been in his own world as he stepped out from between two cars and was killed."

Luke only made a sound, but it was such that she was comforted.

She sighed. "It took a whole year just to notice that life goes on. Then a little longer to realize I was alive and I could live my life again. But I taught, and I couldn't face the kids. We had wanted children, but couldn't have any. To go to school each day and see those darling children, so alive, was torture. I couldn't handle it.

"My family has a solution for insurmountable problems: go nurse the lepers. That is, if you're having problems and finding your life unlivable, then help someone who has worse problems.

"I quit teaching and worked as a soup-kitchen food chopper. When I still couldn't go back to teaching, I got a job as a 'gofer' at the florist." She didn't mention why she left there. She took a deep breath. "I won't ever risk another involvement. It's too much to bear."

Luke said, "I had a similar experience. My wife was sleeping with a friend during the day. She cleaned me out with the divorce. The man was married and had kids. How could I point the finger at him? It would have wrecked his wife. I'd never marry again, either."

"Who'd have you?" Georgia smiled a little. "You're a workaholic! All you think about is business."

"Occasionally, I do have other thoughts." He grinned at her.

He worked hard in his study. The phone rang, he used the computer, Mac brought papers, and then there was Georgia who was the Grasshopper to Luke's industrious Ant.

She was bored and restless. By the third morning of her detention, she again fixed breakfast. Luke appreciated her efforts. Mac came as usual about ten, Luke left. Mac sat down to read the Sunday papers, and that's when she started pacing.

"Where is he today?"

"At the club. He swims."

That made her indignant. Luke got to go swimming and there she was confined to the apartment! It wasn't right.

Indignation forces adrenaline into the bloodstream and it cannot be ignored; it must be used. Georgia sorted out the clothes in the tiny utility room and put one load into the washer. She swept the kitchen floor and made a packaged cake.

Luke came home, looking refreshed from his swim, Mac left, Luke went into his study after lunch, and Georgia was left to her adrenaline.

In folding the second load of dried clothes, Georgia found a rip in one of his pajama tops. His wide shoulders came to her mind. She took her little sewing machine out of its case, set it on her dresser and mended the tear.

Then she went over the rest of the newly laundered clothes, reinforced a seam here and sewed on a button there. After that, she went through all of his clothes.

On Monday, she put her pictures up on the walls. The pictures weren't large, they couldn't be and fit in her little car, but there were more than enough. She lay them out on the floor in the patterns she wanted on the walls.

As always happens with men, the first sound of her hammer brought Luke from his study. "Do you know the chunk your nail holes will take out of my damage deposit?"

"Deduct it from the hundred *thou*," she replied aloofly, "I see no reason not to be comfortable for the next three days."

"Are you so anxious to leave? It could be just a little longer."

"How long?"

"Maybe ten days." His eyes glanced quickly to gauge her reaction.

Did she object? No. She said, "With my financial coup, I shall be off skiing in the Bavarian Alps this winter. Perhaps with a slight bend to the sun down in Rio before going on to Aspen. By then, I shall probably need a job again." She pounded in another nail, "But first I'll need a whole new wardrobe." She gave him a superior look.

"Are you really going skiing?"

"No." She put down the hammer and gave him a glance. "I'll get my doctorate."

"What's your master's in?"

"Art history. With the Ph.D. I could teach college level. I doubt I could ever go back to being with children again."

"Did you do any of these?" He came forward, deliberately changing the subject. Interested, he really looked at the pictures she had up and those arranged on the floor still to be hung.

"Only a few. This one—"

"What is that?" he asked cautiously.

"A druidess."

"I can see the druidess, but what's that with her?"

"Her beast. Druids had beasts. I don't remember them described as anything else, so I used my imagination."

"Are they coming out of that tree?"

"Druids had an affinity with oaks." His reaction to the drawing wasn't very flattering. She lifted her nose.

"Do you have nightmares often?"

"On occasion." She gave him a cool glance. "People with vivid imaginations occasionally have nightmares, but they also have marvelous dreams."

"You dreamed up a dandy with that beast."

"He protects her."

Luke looked up, his smile a bit crooked. "Do you feel the need of a protector?" His strong voice was soft and a little husky.

"I need some exercise! I need to get outside. I am getting a severe case of terminal claustrophobia!"

"I don't dare let you out of here. I could lose you," he said quite honestly.

"You get to swim."

"Yes." He frowned and rubbed his forehead. "Let me see if I can figure a way."

"I'm going berserk with nothing to do."

"Can you use a word processor?" His voice was eager.

"You can't afford me. I draw ten thousand a day."

"Ah, yes. But you're worth it."

She hardly heard that. She was off on a tangent to convince him to let her out. "This apartment is getting smaller every day. *I need exercise!*"

So Mac brought a personal exercise trampoline for in-place running. She loved it, but she turned on MTV to run by, and it drove Luke crazy.

It wasn't long before Mac brought her a cassette player with headphones and the necessary tapes. During her afternoon session on the trampoline, Luke came out after a time and stood next to her until she stopped and unplugged one ear. He told her solemnly, "You need a bra."

"*I* need one?" In disbelief she pulled out her neckline and inspected her chest under the brown terry jumpsuit.

"Maybe looser clothes?" he suggested. Then he decided additionally, "A sack over your head?"

She flopped a dismissive hand, shook her head in amused—pleased—exasperation and turned the trampoline so that he saw only her back. It didn't help him.

As the days passed, Luke had found that he spent more and more of his time sitting at his desk, watching her. He had a clear view of the living room and kitchen. And he watched her every move with lowered eyelids as he lay back in his chair, his body tightening.

He had tried to kiss her the night before, but she'd backed off as if she was scared of him. Her eyes had been enormous. Was he so frightening? Other women had never indicated he was the least bit unattractive. Why would she back off?

Very seriously, she'd said, "Stay away from me."

It had offended him so much that he'd snapped, "I wouldn't touch one of Herb's women with a ten-foot pole!"

And she'd hissed, "I am *not* one of Herb's women!"

"A holdout, huh. What are you asking of him? Will you need it after you get the hundred thousand from me?"

She'd put her hands in her hair and shrieked, "I don't know any Herb!"

Luke rubbed his contented stomach. He was going to have to swim more laps. She'd turned to cooking after his steak dinner. When she'd asked if he had any cookbooks, he'd exclaimed, "You'll do the cooking?"

She'd replied, "I dislike raw meat."

After that, the apartment had been filled with the aroma of baking. Bread, pie, meats, soups; the sound of the mixer or the blender.

She was an amateur.

She'd put too much anise in the pizza yesterday noon, and he could still taste it. She baked bread. When he expressed some astonishment she would try that, she'd replied airily, "Bread is like turkeys."

He'd lifted his head and squinted his eyes as he tried to see the connection, but he hadn't needed to ask, for she went on, "They just take time." So he could nod sagely, as if he understood.

She made two loaves of bread and they turned out two different sizes.

He'd been drawn to the kitchen by the maddening aroma of fresh bread just as she'd lifted the loaves from the oven. She put them on the wire rack to cool and stood back to survey their unmatched forms.

She said, "That's why I'm not in heaven anymore."

He'd said, "Huh?"

"My job in heaven—" she'd sighed "—was making chests. The men's came out all right, but the women's were difficult. They turned out like my bread.''

He looked at the loaves. ''They aren't the same size.''

''That's what God said.'' She looked at him soberly. ''If you see a woman with an unmatched set, she was probably issued a pair of mine.''

It was such a surprise to find that kind of humor in her that it was almost too funny to laugh. So he said equally serious, ''I'll watch for yours.''

But she laughed. And the bread was delicious. Too good. He ate more than was wise.

She put the food on the table for each meal and waited for his reaction. He saw to it that he was unfailingly pleased. His eyes had watered with her chili the first day, but he managed to smile and nod. His throat hadn't worked right for the rest of the day.

Her cheesecake was a masterpiece.

The cucumber soup was weird. The popovers odd. He had been remarkably brave about it all and felt noble.

God only knew what his digestive tract thought had happened to his judgment. He now faced lunch. She'd said it was to be a surprise. That made him brace a little and he'd asked Mac to be sure to come so that he could stay for lunch, and he warned, ''She's cooking. Be kind.''

But then Luke had added, ''Bring an antacid.'' And Mac had given him the stare of one betrayed.

Luke looked through his door at her in the kitchen. She was leaning over frowning at the cookbook Mac had purchased at her direction. She had on a sleeveless yellow terry-cloth pullover and a pair of white shorts. It seemed all his nerves vibrated and his sex tingled with awareness.

She looked like something edible. He would like to have her for lunch. And then dinner. Her skin was so perfect. So smooth. It looked as if it would feel like satin. He longed to touch her. Her mouth was enough to drive a man crazy. She would chew on her lower lip, and he wanted to help.

Her long legs drew his eyes and he wanted to pat her bottom. Her breasts jiggled and looked as if they needed his hands to support them. He was willing to do that. Very willing. He wanted her.

He wanted to make her sigh in his ear as he touched her. He wanted her mouth open and welcoming. He wanted to hold her close and to feel her against him. He wanted to feel her. To put his hands on her and pet and squeeze her. To rub her all over. She was driving him up the wall.

As soon as he'd opened the door to the conference room, he'd seen her, and the shock that had gone through him had stopped him dead in his tracks. Those things didn't happen. He still couldn't believe it had happened to him.

He needed to keep her there long enough so that she could get used to him. He needed her. Why her? And his eyes were drawn to her and he thought it really didn't matter why.

She busily set the drop-leaf table in the living room by the kitchen's dividing counter. She looked at it, then she looked around the apartment. She went out of sight into his bedroom.

She came out and went through a box of her things, leaning over in those shorts. Her breasts hung into the tight shirt, and she was completely unaware of what she was doing to him.

She found a jar someone had made and held it up to look at it critically. It was swirls of blue. She took it over and set it in the middle of the table, then stood back to consider it there. It satisfied her.

He realized that she wanted the table to look nice.

Very busy, she went back to the kitchen. As a courtesy to a houseguest, he decided he should see if he could help her. Such conduct would only be expected. He got up, cast an impatient eye at the papers left on his desk and strolled over to the kitchen counter as if by happenstance. "Need anything done?"

Her face was a little flushed and her hair beginning to tumble from the top of her head. She looked at him vaguely and raised her brows.

He smiled at her. "May I help?"

"A wine. A light white would be nice with the chicken salad. Something with a tingle."

He had enough tingle for a whole case of wine. "I think I have just the thing." He went into the kitchen, reached up past her to open a high cupboard. They were standing a bit close, but she hadn't moved away. She was looking up at his hands.

He had to recall why he was standing there and what he'd been doing. The lunch? Wine. He took down a bottle, then another and a third. He knew very little about wines. Beer, he knew about beer, but wines weren't his drink. He'd always just asked the liquor dealer's opinion. Women liked wine. They felt safe with wine. Luke smiled.

With his big hands, he handled the bottles easily enough. He read the labels and handed the bottles to her, as if she would know what she wanted. He smiled again very nicely.

"Too sweet." She put one back in his hands to be put away. "Either of these would be fine. Which do you prefer?"

The ball back in his court, he handled it: "This one." When in doubt, be positive.

All he had were the small glasses that frozen shrimp cocktails came in. Those were used for the wine.

Mac knocked, was welcomed and Luke felt as if he and Georgia were a couple entertaining a friend. He wondered if she'd stay with him. It would be nice to live with her. They would have to come to some understanding about meals. If they didn't, he'd soon cross the two-hundred-pound mark.

They'd have to do something else to get her out of the kitchen. How about the bedroom? Now, that would be a nice distraction. And for his stomach's sake, he would be willing to distract her. He smiled at her in such a way that she looked a bit startled. He'd have to be more subtle.

"Doesn't the table look nice?" he asked Mac, and nudged Mac's arm with his elbow.

Mac studied the table for a clue and said, "Yeah." With another nudge he added, "Real nice." Then he gave a slanting, inquiring look at Luke.

Georgia served a chicken salad made from last night's roast chicken. There wasn't very much, because it had turned out well the night before and Luke had eaten more than she had expected. He had done that to avoid eating more than two of her biscuits.

Five

There was enough mayonnaise in the chicken salad so that they could swallow it. The meat had been just a little dry. The serving was placed in a cupped Boston lettuce leaf—which tends to be small—and the decoration was a pretty curl of parsley. There was an orange slice and some of the leftover biscuits that had been halved, buttered and sprinkled with sugar and cinnamon before they were toasted.

After each bite, Luke cautiously ran an inquiring tongue over his teeth to assess the damage.

Since the wine bottle was capped, there had been no need for a corkscrew or the ritual of tasting the wine or the chance for cork bits in the first pouring. Luke unscrewed the cap and poured the wine into the shrimp cocktail glasses.

It was Luke who inadvertently started the evaluation of the wine. He wanted to appear knowledgeable to Georgia, so he picked up his glass and swirled the wine a bit before lifting it to his nose. "Nice bouquet."

Mac looked up quickly. In turn, he lifted his own glass. "Umm." He judged noncommittally.

"An elusive fragrance," Luke said inventively. He took a small, testing sip. "Rather sassy." Georgia and Mac watched him with some interest as he took another sip. And he found the word, "Piquant."

Mac tested it and said solemnly, "Somewhat ambiguous."

And Georgia could not resist joining in. She said positively, "Light and airy. It captures summer."

Luke narrowed his eyes thoughtfully. "Just a bit feminine."

Mac har-de-har-harred. Georgia smiled, nicely tolerant. Luke raised his eyebrows, as if Mac had belched as he'd bowed to the Queen.

Then Luke expounded on beers he had known and loved, and Mac talked sipping whiskey. Georgia waxed lyrical over Kellercup strawberry wine, and the two men listened politely.

Neither man had enough to eat, for the chicken was soon gone. "Is there any more? It was delicious," Mac said.

"I'm afraid that's all, but we do have pie for dessert."

"Great!" said Luke. "What kind?"

"A rhubarb pie. It came out a little juicy," Georgia said with some regret.

"Just the way I like it." Luke beamed at her.

However, Mac was a married man and knew not to make rash statements. "Ah, yes, it is kinda—" But Luke leaned forward, cleared his throat and kicked

Mac's shin quite hard. So Mac didn't finish the sentence.

The pie shell wasn't quite done. That sometimes happens with fruit pie. It bubbles and appears finished, but the bottom dough can still be quite raw. Because he'd said he liked juicy pies, Luke got to eat a second piece; while Mac, who'd kept quiet, could pass.

Luke thought Georgia was worth that effort. He saw that her eyes smiled with their compliments and her cheeks pinked so prettily.

And Mac's weighing glances went from one to the other.

Then, as they had plotted, Mac said, "Someone checked on her car."

Luke swung his head around in a snap. "What?"

"My car?" Georgia asked, "Where is my car?"

"They went to the place where we had it stored and asked for a pink car." The two men eyed each other.

"Good thing we decided to have it painted."

"You *painted* it?" she gasped. "How dare you!"

Impatiently Luke replied, "You said you'd paint it a dark green. So, we just did it. It seemed a good time to get it done. Right now you aren't able to drive around and it would just be sitting there. Good thing we did it. It wasn't there." Then Luke asked Mac, "What happened?"

But Georgia exclaimed, "You just arbitrarily took my car and painted it! Without my permission? I don't believe you could be that . . . despotic. It's my car!"

Luke smiled at her. "We'll charge it against the hundred thousand."

"Brilliant!" Mac enthused. "That might have gotten by me."

"I've never been paid for the hamburgers that first night," she said crisply, her cheeks pinker, her voice a little high.

"Deduct it from the paint job," Luke instructed Mac.

"By the time I get away, there probably won't be any of the hundred thousand left! You will devise ways of keeping it all. I bet I'm even paying rent on that room!"

"Hey! Good idea!" Mac took a notebook from his pocket and clicked a pen into place.

"Have you checked with the IRS about her, Mac? Will the expenses we incur be deductible? A business expense? Entertainment?"

"EnterTAINment!" She was indignant.

Luke soothed her. "You'll make a mint selling this experience to *Ms* or *Woman's World* or something like that. Other women can read it and get hostile and not speak to their husbands or boyfriends and there will be all kinds of ramifications." Then he asked Mac, "Do they know who it was at storage? Any description?"

"Fake. They had rented a truck and the panel was a taped-on cardboard. They found that later."

"What reason did they give for wanting the pink car?"

"They had the name right." The two men exchanged a studiedly sober look, then Mac added, "They said the car was to be cleaned and the paint touched up."

"So we know who it was."

"Yeah."

"Herb?" she asked. "This nemesis?"

"You're safe with us," Luke said so staunchly that Mac choked.

"I'm being hunted because of you!" She was cross, and oddly not in the least alarmed. Herb was a part of this whole incident, which was so incredible that how could she consider it as serious? Aloud she said, "This is all too ridiculous. None of it can be real."

"Herb's a lady-killer. He can get any woman to do anything he wants . . . like steal secrets. Or tell them."

"I didn't steal any secrets! I did not come there because of Herb. I am just moving to Indianapolis. I may change my mind about that. If you two are any indication of what the people in Indianapolis are like, perhaps I should find another place!" Her voice was becoming a little shrill.

"Now, Georgia—" Luke began.

"Don't you 'now, Georgia' me! I've had as much idiocy as I can take. I have never been involved in anything remotely resembling this, and I find it unsettling."

"Of course you do." Mac was sympathetic.

"Don't take that tone with me!"

Luke inquired, "How would your mother cope with these circumstances?"

She looked blankly at him and then shook her head before she smiled. "I suppose she would love it."

"Are you a daddy's girl? Or can you draw on her genes, too? Enjoy this unique opportunity as a chance to see another facet of life."

"Excellent." Mac was impressed.

Georgia said, "Well, I don't actually believe she would relax and enjoy it, I believe she would devise all sorts of dramatic escape plots."

"Forget your mother," Luke advised hastily. "Maybe I could figure a way for you to swim each day."

"No, you can't." Mac was emphatic. "Herb has a constant watch on you. They know you brought her here. She can't be anywhere else. If you two start running in and out of the house swimming and playing golf, don't you suppose someone will notice?"

"Okay, Mac, you've made the point."

"They're probably planning right this minute to mount a full-scale attack on this place to carry her off!"

"Now, Mac..."

"Attack?" Georgia's voice was rather thin.

"Don't panic," Luke advised. "Herb isn't totally dumb. And he's more subtle than that."

"Attack?" Georgia was still snagged on that word.

"Don't worry about a thing. Mac just needs a good night's sleep. When he's tired, he sees spooks."

"You blame everything on Penny," Mac objected with indignation.

"Penny's afraid to leave you any energy, in case you'd look around. She's insecure."

"I'm irresistible." Mac lowered his eyes modestly.

Luke was reassuring. "Mac, with our own security and the patrols here at the complex, there is no need for alarm."

"I wasn't alarmed, I was worried," Mac explained.

"What about this attack?" Georgia took them back to that word. "Tell me about this."

"They create a distraction, come in and snatch you so they can find out all you know about the Molly Q.

Time is fleeting. There're only about five days left..."
And he stopped and frowned at her.

"Five days? I thought this was only going to be a week."

"It might be just a little longer. And we have to be careful of Herb's craftiness in getting to you."

"People don't actually do that sort of thing," she scoffed.

"Every day in the newspapers. People read about it and say, 'How astonishing.' And they say, 'Who'd ever think something like that could happen?' Or they say, 'That won't ever happen to me.' Then when it does happen, like now, some little snoop says, 'People don't really do that sort of thing.'"

Mac corrected, "She said 'actually.'"

"Actually," Luke corrected himself.

"I'll scrub the kitchen floor." She looked at Mac as if communicating, but he'd forgotten that had been his solution when she'd first complained about not having anything to do and wanted to exercise.

"What did you do to the kitchen floor?" Luke frowned at Mac.

"I wasn't even in there!" Mac protested.

"For exercise." Georgia sighed and put a hand to her forehead to comfort herself.

Luke smiled at her. "We could open the table out all the way, put it in the middle of the floor and I could chase you around it! How about that? We could set up forfeits for losing and have a lot of fun. Good exercise!"

"We could play table tennis!"

Luke frowned. "That's kid stuff."

Mac said in derision, "He means he can't play well enough to beat you, so he disparages the game."

"He'd do that?"

"Every time."

"I'll play left-handed." Luke looked grudgingly cooperative.

Mac blabbed: "He is left-handed."

"You tell everything you know."

"You have to be fair." Mac was reasonable. "She's your guest."

"She's my *captive,* and she's supposed to do what I want."

"Careful there, Montana. Things could get out of hand."

"Can you belly dance?" Luke asked her. "While I'm not too enthusiastic about table tennis, I wouldn't mind having to watch a little belly dancing."

"I don't belly dance."

"Ah! Here's the opportunity for you to learn a new skill. Mac, see if you can find a do-it-yourself book on it and you'd have to get the accoutrements. The ruby for her belly button, the scarves, that sort of thing."

Mac said, "Well—"

Georgia said, "No."

Luke objected to Mac, "I have put my mind to the problem of her exercising, and I don't get any credit! She turns down all my suggestions and then complains because she hasn't any way to exercise."

"I am going crazy cooped up in here with a madman—"

"Going? You're there!" He turned indignantly to Mac. "Have you noticed all the pictures on the walls? She—"

Mac looked around. "It really looks nice."

"Thank you."

Luke groused. "Do you know what that's going to do to my damage deposit? She's ruining the walls, demanding all sorts of privileges, being hard to get along with—"

"I am *not* hard to get along with! Once you adjust to my way of doing things, I can be very agreeable." She tilted back her head as Mac laughed.

"Women!"

Mac pushed back his chair and stood up. "Thank you so much for sharing your lunch with me. I must go. Is there anything I can get for you, Georgia?"

"Freedom."

"Now, Georgia—" Luke began.

Mac suggested, "How about something easier?"

"Nothing else." She did have some of her mother's genes, for she managed to look pale and persecuted. She did it well.

So well that Luke frowned as he watched her.

As Mac left, he repeated to Luke, "Be careful."

Again alone with her, Luke did try to go into the study and tackle the papers waiting for him, but he found himself carrying dishes from the table over to the counter and clearing the table.

She allowed that. She put the dishes into the dishwasher and there still weren't enough to wash a load. She straightened the kitchen, then left him standing there as she went with slow, aimless little steps into the living room, picked up Minny and sat down with the cat on her lap.

Luke trailed along as if led by a string. "Would you like to play some cribbage?"

She sighed gently. "No, thanks."

He sat down and racked his brain for interesting, intriguing conversation. It wasn't readily at hand.

"Georgia. A southern name. Mine's Montana and that's a Yankee name. You ever hear about us Yankees marching through Georgia?"

"Montana was only a territory during the war between the States. It didn't enter the Union until twenty years or so after that." Then she made her face sad and gently chided, "And to tease about Marching through Georgia is something like being derisive about the Alamo."

"Where in the south is your home?"

"Near Cleveland."

"Ohio?"

She smiled just a little.

"You deliberately backed me into a corner! You wicked, wicked woman." And his yellow eyes glinted with the fires that were no longer safely banked.

On that Tuesday afternoon, which was the fifth day of her captivity, a florist delivered a stunning bouquet of pink roses, pink carnations and baby's breath. Luke took it at the door, and when it was closed he turned to her with that mass of flowers hiding the upper half of his body and said, "This is for you. I know the apartment is gloomy for you, with all this rain. For me, you are the bouquet. So this is for you. Pink and lacy, for a lady."

Having worked for a florist, Georgia knew how much he'd spent on the flowers, and she was shocked by such a squandering of money. Men tended to elaborate when all they really needed was a token. Three roses and some baby's breath would have been just as effective. What did she mean: effective?

Exclaiming prettily over it, she had him place it on the coffee table by the sofa, and Minny watched with minimal interest. The bouquet covered most of the table. Luke waited. Why? Did he expect her to throw her arms around him, kiss him and drag him down on the carpet in gratitude?

She smiled and said "Thank you," and he forced himself to nod his head once in what he hoped was gracious acknowledgment. Then he disciplined himself to go back to the study.

She spent the afternoon working on some needlepoint, running on the trampoline and organizing a casserole of baked pork chops, with canned tomatoes, peas and rice that was a no-fail recipe of her mother's and guaranteed to please the heart of any man. She combined the liquid from the tomatoes with onions, mustard and a bit of Worcestershire sauce, and poured it over the meat, vegetables, and rice before she put it to bake.

She scraped the rhubarb out of the remainder of the unsatisfactory pie shell, put it in bowls to be topped with whipped cream after it cooled in the refrigerator. Luke had scored points with his kindness over the pie.

Her eyes went often to the flowers, and she was quite charmed by the man.

That night, when Luke told Georgia good-night, he kissed her. He didn't hold her to him, he simply leaned over and his warm, chiseled, softened lips touched hers in an exquisitely gentle salute. Actually, it wasn't anything to write home about as an actual kiss. It was short, sweet and . . . excessively erotic. And she was a long, sighing time getting to sleep that night.

He wanted an affair. That was obvious. He wanted to sleep with her. He was attracted. He wanted no complications. Just an intimate relationship with no ties.

Why not? It had been so long. She was shocked how her body reacted to the idea. To thinking of his body. Why his? There had been other men who had been interested to varying degrees, from comforting the widow to actually liking her as a woman and wanting to give her pleasure, too.

But she had never been willing. She had been free of this sweet turmoil for two years. Why now with this man? Luke Montana.

Since Georgia hadn't slept well after Luke gave her his insidious little, non-touching, good-night kiss, she was forced to take a nap that afternoon of her sixth day.

The rain had returned and the gloomy coolness made napping very nice.

She was lying there, disgruntled with her relentless imagination for plotting his seduction, when there was an odd little scratching knock on the apartment door.

It got her out of bed and listening suspiciously at her own closed door. She heard Luke walk across the living-room carpet, knew he looked through the peephole, and she heard him turn the knob and open the door.

A salacious feline voice said, "Hi, darling."

"Sharon," he acknowledged briefly.

"Aren't you going to let me come inside?"

"I'm really very busy. What did you want?"

"Well, you could be a little more welcoming, darling."

"Cut it out."

"You're prickly today! I know just the thing to relax you." She laughed a throaty chuckle that was wicked.

"What are you doing?"

"I'm just getting comfortable. What's the matter, Luke. Aren't you—"

"Now wait a minute, Sharon—"

"What is *that?*"

As busy as Georgia was by then, even she heard Minny hiss. All that hiss came out of that little cat?

"Luke! You know I don't like cats. Put it outside!"

"In the rain?" He was aghast.

It was then, with calculation and patting a fake yawn, that Georgia chose to open her bedroom door and stand posed.

She'd ripped off the T-shirt she used for sleeping and put on a soft green lawn cotton scoop-necked, sleeveless mid-hip-length shift over matching briefs that had soft ruffles across the bottom of her bottom. It was an excessively flirty, naughty outfit. And it exposed a lot of Georgia to the unstrained imagination.

"Who are you?" The dulcet voice had turned shockingly harsh.

"Could you guys keep it down a little?" Georgia stretched a tad elaborately. "I need my sleep if tonight's going to be anything like last night, Tiger." She gave Luke a slow, lazy smile.

"Who is this woman?" the newcomer demanded of Luke.

Luke never moved his avid stare from Georgia. "My cousin?"

"Cousin!" Both women exclaimed at once. Sharon in disbelief, and Georgia in amused delight.

Georgia asked Sharon sympathetically, "Did he lead you astray . . . too?"

Sharon snarled something vicious, picked up her jacket, having to pull it out from under Minny who stayed on it long enough to annoy the woman. Sharon held the jacket by thumb and forefinger and stomped out, slamming the door.

Luke went slowly to Georgia, who said, "I just saved you from that witch! You owe me."

Not really paying close attention to his words, he told her: "It's part of the hundred thousand. A package deal. Our agreement says in the fine print that you are to protect me from predatory women during your stay here. You did it magnificently." He hugged her close against him, her soft body finally crushed against the hardness of his.

He growled in her ear in a low, throaty menace, "Where did you get that outfit? All I've ever seen on you has been jogging outfits and T-shirts. That's mind-boggling."

"I made it."

"Talents to spare! You draw, mend and sew. Amazing." He hadn't mentioned cooking as a talent.

But she wasn't paying any real attention to words, she was vividly aware of Luke. Of his body against hers. Of his arms holding her. Of his breath hot on the side of her throat. Of his availability.

She was going wild inside. Her hands moved on his shoulders as she pressed against him. Her tongue did Minny touches to his throat, as she inhaled his masculine scent. It had been too long.

He kissed her. He really kissed her. He sampled her mouth, exploring it, savoring it, sharing his. She be-

gan to moan and she couldn't prevent the little movements of her hungry body. She could have him.

His hands scrubbed over the soft material, seeking
the shape of her. Her breasts moved in his clutching
hands and her back arched. He made marvelously
erotic sounds in his throat as he kissed her. His hands
went to her back and slid down her spine's curve in
pleasure, cupping her ruffle-clad bottom, bringing her
tightly to him.

In every way she helped him to seduce her. There
was no hesitation. No second thoughts. She wanted
him. She gave him no time to reconsider. She unbuttoned his shirt and lost two buttons in her frantic
hurry. One pinged against the wall, and his laugh only
encouraged her.

Somehow, she was naked. When had he taken off
her top? Her panties were gone. She was standing
there completely nude, locked against him, and struggling to stay against him as she undressed him.

As intent as she was in getting him out of his
clothes, she was too slow for him. He helped. Then he
lay her down on the carpet, feasting his eyes, touching her, running his hands along her, smoothing her
silky skin, leaning to suckle her, to touch his tongue to
her. He drove her mad.

Her fingers dug into his shoulders trying to get him
closer, to get him to come to her, to make him take her.
And he did. There on the carpet, he covered her with
his big, strong body and he filled her, making love to
her.

But he wasn't too distracted not to protect her. "Are
you on the pill?"

"No."

"No?" he asked in disbelief. And he had to get up and search, then put on his trousers and go out to his car, before he found something to use. By then she was almost climbing the wall. He laughed deep in his throat. His yellow eyes burning with golden fires of desire.

He took her to his bed, the big wide bed made for love, for the tumble and turning and madness of ardent writhings of their sexual dance.

Their kisses were hot and melting. She went light-headed as she made squeaking gasps of need.

Sweat filmed their bodies as they worked at love, and she—in her need—became aggressive and began her own torment of him. And she laughed as he gasped and his breath became labored.

And when at last they surrendered, their flight was fantastic as they lifted to the peak, to hesitate before their thrilling ecstasy carried them on to magic, to sweet fulfillment.

She wept. Little helpless sounds. He leaned over her, smoothing back her sweat-dampened hair, asking, "What is it? Are you all right?" She nodded. "I didn't hurt you, did I?" She shook her head. "I really got a little wild. You drove me crazy. My God, Georgia, you are fantastic! What's the matter, honey? Shh, now. Don't cry."

How could she say she grieved because she had never had such a marvelous experience with Phillip? She had never given Phillip such pleasure. Their sex had been nice. But never had it been the mind-blowing paradise she'd just shared in Luke's arms. After Luke had made such love to her, how could she distress him by telling him that she grieved for her husband?

Six

Georgia controlled her tears and told Luke his love-making was beautiful. She even managed to tease him about his desperate search for protection.

"Well, with Mac popping in and out, I never thought we'd be able to." He lay there propped on one elbow next to her, and one big hand slowly rubbed circles on her stomach.

"I thought Mac said this apartment was like an office, and this sort of thing never happens in offices." Her lashes were spiked with her tears, and her face was pale. It made her smile and teasing words all the more heart-touching.

He leaned to kiss her, his lips soft and sweet. "This room isn't an office. I think I'll barricade the doors for a couple of months."

She liked having her stomach rubbed that way. Then his big, hard hand moved, and she liked it on her breasts, as well. On her face, her thighs, down her arms, her back, her bottom: his hands relished her.

His kisses were varied, tasting her mouth, her breasts, sipping, nipping, using his tongue. His mouth was scalding and his breath steamed. His breathing was becoming rapid, like a long-distance runner who was a little out of shape.

She thought she was simply lying there, allowing his delight in her, but then she noticed her own hands were off on all sorts of adventures, and she adjusted to his interests, tilting, pressing, turning.

Her body had softened invitingly, her breasts were full and lush, her hips moved minutely to entice. Her mouth explored him. Her tongue tasting, teasing, as her teeth rubbed here and there.

The first time had been lust too-long-held, this was enticement. This was pleasure taken and given lavishly, in mutual appreciation.

How could there be so many ways to kiss? To touch one place? How interesting to find that while gentle touches were needed to begin, as their heat rose, rougher touches were exciting, as they were interspaced with the petting ones. How amazing were the varied positions and the prolonging of the completion. How lovely it was for a man and a woman to make love. If she was enthralled, so was he.

When they were sated, he didn't want to let got of her. His hands were drawn to her. Hands touching. His mouth wanted more. Mouths touching. His glances had trouble leaving her. His eyes smiled.

"We should dress. Mac—"

He kissed her yet again.

"You are amazing."

"You, too."

Their conversation went on that way for a long while. The phone rang in the office, and he reluctantly got up to answer it. What excuse could they have for not answering a phone? What *other* excuse?

She watched him walk across the room to the door. His marvelous male body was so beautiful. He should be forbidden to wear clothes. He paused at the door. "Don't go away." And he smiled at her.

She turned her gaze to the window to the new sunshine after such a long rainy spell. Was this a sign? Her life, too, had long been in gloom and would she now be able to face life and love it again? Love living? Poor Phillip. Had he ever experienced anything like she'd just had? In any of life's facets, had he ever been fulfilled?

Not with her. Not with music. Not with any job he'd had. Not ever? How dreadfully sad. And her eyes filled again.

"I can only assume you're weeping because I've been away from you?" But his eyes were concerned.

She stretched up her arms and took him down on her and she hugged him to her with all her might. He made a purring sound in his chest and scooped his hands under her to wrap her close to him.

"Can you tell me why you're crying?"

"I've never felt this way. I've been moved by music and by art and by words, but I've never cried before when making love. You are a phenomenon." He hugged her more tightly, and she said, "When I get my hundred thousand, I'll set up a factory and bottle you and sell you at outrageous prices to lonely ladies."

"Are you lonely?"

"Most people are. We just don't all realize it. When other people admit to being lonely, it astonishes us.

Mary Tyler Moore. Linda Evans. How amazing such well-known people could ever be lonely. It is a lesson to us all that they would admit to loneliness. It makes the rest of us less so. And it makes us know we have to fill our own lives. 'Go nurse the lepers.''' She laughed, a little self-consciously. "End of lecture."

"You need me."

"I've enjoyed you," she corrected. "Let me up, you enormous lug, I'm being crushed. I must bathe and dress. So must you."

"Since this is a day of new experiences, I'll bathe you."

She scoffed, unbelieving that he'd never bathed a woman before.

"Come on, show me how. I think it's something that I could take up and do well."

There was no discouraging him. He was interested. "Under normal circumstances, I suppose I would have to remove her clothing first?"

She gave him a patient look.

"I can figure out turning on water and having soap handy, but what do women wash first?"

"It could vary." She lectured with some broadness. "For instance, there are people who eat dessert first."

"I should wash you there first?"

So they began, and he found she was ticklish, but so was he; and they laughed and played. "I thought you were burned out?"

"You've saved me!"

And she laughed.

After supper, when Mac came by to bring the mail from the office, Luke had to thrust his hands in his pockets to keep from touching Georgia. Georgia's eyes danced, and she laughed too easily.

It was an amusing plight. After making such love, they had to be sated. They'd spent the afternoon playing and teasing, indulging their senses, making love. But they wanted to touch. They wanted to gaze into each other's eyes and smile. They wanted to whisper all sorts of things to each other. Intimate, teasing things. They wanted to go back to Luke's big bed and lie in each other's arms, rub against one another and sigh.

This new distracting attraction had mesmerized them, and they wanted more. Their gazes met and their bodies knew it all through them. It was exciting. They found casual excuses to touch or brush, their glances caught and they smiled their laughter.

They found even inconvenience thrilling, for after Mac left, they would be alone again. They looked at each other. Luke's yellow eyes were golden with his interest. And she gently sank her teeth into her bottom lip and watched his reaction.

Mac saw that and continued, observant, unnoticed by the pair. He opened the cookie jar, catching their attention. Mac cautiously tested a molasses one. He chewed critically, as they waited, and lifted his brows in surprise. "Hmm," was all Mac said, but he had another one.

Luke poured himself a glass of milk and lifted it and his brows to Georgia to see if she wanted one. She shook her head. So he sat down next to her, across from Mac and drank the milk as he, too, ate cookies.

Around a half-chewed bite, but neatly, Mac asked, "How's he behaving?" And he gave Georgia a level look.

She went scarlet from toes to scalp.

Luke volunteered smugly. "I'm behaving superbly."

"I asked her."

"Superbly." But she coughed a little.

"Getting tired of me butting in, yet?"

Georgia gasped, but Luke laughed. He said, "We look forward to your company."

"Losing your touch?"

"Mac," he complained. "You owe your job to me. You're supposed to be kind and courteous and respectful."

This idea hit Mac's funny bone and he laughed and choked, and they had to pound his back. So much for respect.

Without looking at either of his watchers, Mac said, as if practiced, "There's been some odd queries of the office personnel. As always, they've reported it, described the people, place and time. It's about her." Mac pointed to Georgia. "They ask about a pink car. Say they're looking for a girl in a pink car, who is wanted for questioning in a robbery. Parker says they're not looking for anyone like her."

Georgia asked, "Who is Parker?"

"He's in our security."

Luke accepted that it was so: "Herb."

"Probably."

"What sort of people were they?" Luke asked.

"Nice, clean-cut, FBI-type."

Luke nodded. "Herb."

"I put a couple of people outside. Very discreetly. You won't see them unless you need them."

"That's probably best."

"What's this all about?" Georgia blurted. "People don't actually do this sort of thing!"

Her table companions only gave her an impatient glance.

Minny came in sleepily and jumped up on Luke's lap to be fed tidbits.

Stiffly Georgia chided, "I never feed Minny at the table."

No one paid any attention to her.

After a silence that was not an easy one, because she could almost hear their thinking about her as a problem, Georgia asked, "Am I really in danger? We could go to the police."

"They don't have the time. Nor the manpower. We've got it under control." Mac had another cookie.

"Is there really any danger?" Georgia was persistent.

"Not with us around. Just don't go outside."

"I am getting claustrophobic."

"We'll get her some travel tapes for the VCR." Mac stood up and stretched. "Don't stay up too late, children." And he left.

Georgia looked at Luke. "What is really going on?"

Very openly, Luke replied, "Herb has a network that you wouldn't believe. We are excellent antagonists. Matched. They saw that pink car of yours parked by my building all that time, and they got curious. I would bet anything that's what happened."

"Will I ever see my car again?"

"Of course! When this is over."

"Is there any —real danger?" she asked it, yet again.

"Herb wants to know what we're doing," Luke replied handily. "Since you were only supposed to deliver a letter, and he could know you did by backtracking on your trail, he knows there's some reason we didn't let you go. He wants to talk to you.

By now he knows I'm not at the office, and I wouldn't be on vacation at this time, with things so close, so he knows we're together, and he would love to get his hands on you. We can't risk that." Luke appeared completely logical.

"Would he . . . kill me?"

"Of course not." Luke scoffed at such an idea. "Whatever you've seen or heard, we would know by now." Luke elaborated: "He'd be curious about what you know. If he could get his hands on you, then he would find out everything."

"Would he hurt me?"

"He won't get you. As long as you stay inside with me or Mac, you're all right."

Minny had vanished. It was getting late. They'd had a physically exhausting afternoon of love. They should get to bed. They couldn't bring themselves to move. They sat at the kitchen table and held hands.

Finally he reached lazily and scooped her gently into his arms and onto his lap. And he kissed her sweetly, gently. He'd never felt this need before to hold and keep. It wasn't yet an acknowledged possessiveness. He only recognized his need for her to be close to him.

He stood, still holding her, and carried her to bed. They were contented to sleep in each other's arms.

She dreamed of Phillip that night. It was the first time in a long, long while. And she wakened the next morning feeling guilty and somewhat depressed. Luke wasn't there beside her. She got up, but she didn't go in search of him. Having showered and dressed, still pensive, she went into the living room.

Luke came from the study. He was totally concentrated on Georgia, but she felt a little shy with him. He said, "I want you to realize I've stayed away from you so that you could sleep."

She went to him. Her arms held him almost with anguish, and when he lifted his head to look at her, her self-conscious laugh wasn't quite steady.

His voice was very tender, "Are you suddenly afraid of me?"

She buried her face into his shoulder and shook her head as she denied it. "How could I be?"

"What is it?"

How could she describe it to him? How could she form all the words to explain another man, so that Luke would understand—when she did not?

It was a telling thing that his arms turned cherishing as he held her. The sounds in his throat were soothing, comforting, reassuring. He'd be a fabulous father...

Children? Why had that thought come along? But Luke would be a perfect father. Luke should have children.

"Did I hurry you too much yesterday?" Luke lifted his head and petted her hair back from her face. It was such a tender thing to do.

"It was beautiful."

His kiss was so sweet. "Any second thoughts?"

"No second thoughts." She looked up at him, still a little shy.

"I sent Mac to Terre Haute to check something out for me."

She leaned back in his arms to ask, "Why did you do that?"

"I thought we'd like to be alone."

"Ah-h-h." She was elaborately astonished. And she laughed. "I'm starved."

"Good."

"For food." She chided, but she laughed again.

"You . . . you're mortal?"

"Very."

So he fixed her an enormous breakfast. And he was patient, watching her eat.

"You remind me of a tomcat we had, who watched the feline in heat and just waited."

"Are you in heat?"

"Not anymore."

He kissed her very nicely. He touched and questioned, "How does that feel?" and she would say, "Uh . . ." And he would say, "Good. We're making progress." And he removed her clothing and shed his own.

He would tell her, "Let me know what you like. *A*, or *B*, or *C*." And he'd touch her. She'd say, "Uh . . ." He would say, "I like *C*, too." And he carried her back to bed.

His fingerprints from that first day's grasp were now a greeny-yellow on her arm, and he again kissed them to make them well. But then he kissed a lot of places that had never been harmed and had no bruises.

He gently rubbed his prickly morning whiskers across her full breasts, peaking the nipples for his mouth. Their excited bodies became vividly sensitive to each touch, eager for the other, hurting with wanting.

He moved back slowly so that he could look at her, lying on his bed, and her gaze, too, feasted on him. She smiled into the golden fires of his eyes, and thought again that he invited her to him with the feeling she wouldn't be burned.

His glances then dropped down her body, and she slowly turned, posing for him. Pleasuring his eyes. Her long legs were sleek and smooth, her breasts full like fruit on her slender torso. The indentation of her navel, an accent mark that invited his touch. Her hips were smooth and elegant, her bottom sassy. And his eyes turned smoky.

She slowly put her hands up and lifted her hair with her wrists and allowed it to spread over her pillow in a gesture that entranced him. And he smiled as he watched her intently.

It thrilled him that she would deliberately entice him, and he had to hold her. He was oddly tender with her, as aroused as she had him.

Her face was serious, her eyes wide. She wasn't practiced in this art. Her arms were up, her hands above her head on the bed, the palms up in an uncalculated gesture of surrender. She was a little modest and that was the impulse that made her slightly raise one knee. She didn't know how feminine, how tempting she looked.

IIc did. He began to make slow love to her. However, she twitched and squeaked and gasped. That hurried him along more quickly than he wanted to go.

She excited him to an extreme. He would lift his head to take deep breaths, which should have helped, but she had her fingers in his body hair and tugged at him.

When she became fevered, what was he to do? They fused, entangled, and she murmured when he filled her as she desired. She stretched under him, putting her arms and legs spread-eagled on that big bed as he took possession of her. Then she curled her body to him, locking her heels around him, her hands enclosed his head as her fingers dug through his hair into his scalp, and her teeth grazed his lips and then his shoulder.

It was fantastic. How could mere mortals deign to seek the pleasures of the old gods? How dared they? But they did. As if it was their right, they took all the sensual feelings so lavishly filling them and savored them all.

They hesitated as they reached the zenith, and their gazes caught. It was a strangely solemn exchange. Then he leaned slowly to kiss her almost chastely in that maelstrom of emotion, before he moved, taking her with him to paradise.

It was almost noon when Mac came with the requested papers from nearby Terre Haute and went into the study with Luke. Georgia was sleepily reading, curled in a big overstuffed chair by the window in the living room, with Minny sprawled on her lap.

From the study, she could hear Mac say in sudden heat, "She's vulnerable. You have to be careful of her."

"I know what I'm doing. Quit being such a worry-wart."

"You don't understand women," Mac declared. "You have to be careful of them."

"And you understand them?"

"A hell of a lot better than you do!"

Then one of them hushed the other, and their voices became just a rumble to Georgia. There really was danger? It seemed so impossible.

She put her head on the high back of the chair and looked pensively out the window. This whole situation was very strange. And marvelous. Who would ever think two people could experience such rapture?

If it hadn't been for this weird encounter, she would have gone through her life convinced novelists had impossible imaginations.

She thought of Phillip and sighed, as she looked out the window.

"Don't tell me," Mac's low voice boomed nearby. "You want Chinese."

She and Minny both stretched, and Georgia smiled at Mac. "It's just being inside so long and only seeing the sun. I'm deteriorating."

"Deteriorating!" Luke was shocked.

"Us plants need sunlight or we wilt and shrivel away."

That's why she and Minny found themselves on the roof that afternoon. It was tar paper with white gravel, which could be ruined by walking on it. She would probably have to use most of her hundred thousand to replace the roof. It would be worth the money.

She ran the perimeter of it, laughing and waving her arms as if she was demented.

Luke cautioned, "Shh. Don't advertise."

Minny prowled, walking the short lip of the roof, peering into the surrounding trees and down to the ground.

"If you have to get back to work, I promise I won't jump into the trees and run away." She smiled at him.

"I prefer to stand here and watch you run. You jiggle."

"I do not! I'm all firm muscle!" She swaggered over. "Feel." And her look was naughty.

So he did. But she pushed away, laughing and jogged the circuit, exuberant to be outside, under the blue sky and hot August sun.

She was enjoying it so much, that he couldn't stand still, so he trotted with her, pacing her easily. They sprinted, and he kept up, then he simply ran away from her. He was astonishing.

When she was nicely tired, she stretched and moved and walked to cool down, then he took her back to his apartment, bathed her and they slept.

Georgia sat up in bed, "Minny!"

They both pulled on clothing and retrieved the little cat from the roof. She hadn't minded and didn't quarrel at them for forgetting her.

Luke didn't get much work done. It was too tempting to be together, to watch each other and smile as they laughed over things that weren't all that funny.

"Of all the things in this world, what do you hate the most?"

"I would assume," he said, "that we aren't talking world situations, pollution, human rights?"

"No."

"Those do tend to distract from the petty things, but I suppose paperwork is the bane. What's yours?"

"Cleaning kitchen cupboards."

"That must be a biggie, if you didn't have to choose."

"I can put that off the easiest of all. What do you like best?"

"You."

"That was an excellent, PR-calculated reply. Other than me. And sex."

"Living. This is a wondrous world."

"Phillip didn't find it so."

"I pity him."

"Have you ever in your life not had what you wanted?"

He realized their frivolous conversation had taken a subtle, more meaningful turn, and her question wasn't a casual one. "Everyone has disappointments. No one is immune. Anyone who reaches out is going to miss now and then."

"Or all the time."

"Then you adjust your goals." He said that as he rose from the sofa to answer the phone.

"Georgia!" he called. "It's your father."

She ran to the phone and stood there to say, "Well, hello! Is everything all right?"

"Fine," said her dad's gravelly voice. "It was time for you to check in. The Gradys hadn't heard from you, and I just wondered if you're all right. Who's the guy?"

Her gaze lifted to Luke standing, listening, too, and his face went blank, as he wondered how she would reply.

"My boss. I'm helping him with some research." She gave Luke a precious smile, and he had to clap a hand over his mouth to stop the blurt of surprise.

"What sort of research?"

"It's temporary. How's the family? How's mother's play going?"

"She's playing a Lassie-type dog's 'mother' with a mostly stuffed collie and a whining sound track. The play is actually *Raggs to the Rescue,* and there's an asinine little boy who's so talented, when he's on the stage, that everybody can almost endure him otherwise. He'll probably go to films next. Over there in Indiana. The film business is getting really big there, did you know that?"

"No. How's she to live with, as Raggs's 'mother'?"

"Pure." He sighed.

They laughed, then Georgia said, "I've got to go, Dad. I'll check in again soon. Give my love to everyone and to you."

"Take care, honey."

She hung up the phone and turned to Luke.

"You didn't squeal."

"I'm committed to this caper." She flicked imaginary ashes from a nonexistent cigar.

But she'd been startled by his comment, and he had seen that she was. It hadn't occurred to her that the phone call had been an opportunity to escape. All she had to say was: help. But she hadn't. It shocked her. It thrilled him.

By then he took her into his arms as easily as if he'd been doing it forever, as if he had that right. And she allowed it. She liked it. She needed it.

But it worried her. There was that nagging little memory of Luke's first wife, who had been unfaithful, and whose divorce had cleaned him out. He had said he wouldn't try marriage again.

Marriage? Who had said anything about marriage? She wasn't having anything more to do with it, either! It could hurt too terribly.

Live for the day. That had been her motto for over a year. Ever since she'd emerged from the long depression after Phillip's death, realized the world was still working and it was only Phillip who had died.

For dinner, they had chicken Oriental—with pineapple, mushrooms, peas and Chinese cabbage. There were meringue cookies and Jell-O for dessert. Luke was pleased because he thought she was watching his weight.

They sat at the table in shorts and T-shirts, bare-footed in the August evening. She said, "I doubt this would qualify as truly 'Chinese,' but I thought I noted a bit of pensiveness and I wanted you to feel cherished."

His smile warmed her. Then he reminded her, "It's more than just eating Chinese food from the deli, if you recall Mac's solution for Penny's pensiveness. He added a large dose of hanky-panky."

"Do you mean hamburgers would have done the trick just as well as Chinese food? That it's the hanky-panky that's the main ingredient?"

"It's not having to fix supper and therefore having the energy to indulge in a little fooling around."

"Ahh," she said in realization.

"When do you start the rest of the solution to my pensiveness?"

"You're not the least bit pensive," she scoffed. "I was being funny. I wanted to see if I could fix this, because the picture in the cookbook is gorgeous. I really don't like pineapple with chicken."

He put his chin on his big hand and looked out across the living room through the windows to the evening light, and he sighed—pensively.

She leaned back in delighted laughter, then bent forward to reach out one hand to push on his shoulder.

He turned dancing eyes to her and reached up a thumb and forefinger to take his lower lip and shake it as he said, "It's really a jungle out there. You have no idea the cost in stress."

"Hey!" she exclaimed in congratulation. "Almost word for word! That's talent."

He gave her a forebearing look and scolded pensively, "You're supposed to put your hand on my shoulder and say my name in your special voice." He waited.

She sobered elaborately, rivaling Liv Ullman's "compassion" as she put her hand on his shoulder and said, "Mac?"

"Mac!" he roared.

She fled to the bedroom door, but she couldn't hold it against him, and she struggled and giggled and squealed. She released the door and ran over the bed, through the bathroom and on through into the living room, to the other side of the table, as Minny watched their cat-and-mouse game with professional critique.

"Hold still!" he commanded. "This is supposed to be the hanky-panky part."

"Nonsense. You're not in the least pensive. Look at you! Eager, beady-eyed, stalking me around this table! Pensive is sitting down, dull-eyed and pining."

He straightened, strode over to the fat couch, flung himself down in a very dangerous semi-crouch, looking as if he could spring clear across the living room in a single bound, and he pinned her with his fiery look.

She laughed.

Seven

Luke's own amusement bubbled, but he tried to hold his grin under control. He licked his lips like a lion whose stomach is beginning to growl and there's a handy wildebeest nearby... or was his hunger for a lioness who was teasing him?

He leaned back and said, "The dinner was delicious. You did a great job."

"Why, thank you, kind sir." Georgia stuck one fingertip into her cheek to make a dimple. There might have been more of her mother in her than she'd ever realized.

He snatched up a magazine from the couch and flipped it open. "There's an article I've been meaning to show you, come look."

She laughed a cascade of delight. "In *Sports Illustrated?*"

He gave her a lofty look. "Lots of women like sports."

"And you're a sport?"

"I thought you said this apartment was closing in on you! You're getting very sassy, do you realize that? How far do you think you can run?"

She swaggered. "Far enough."

He lunged up from the couch, and she squealed and fled. He gave her the opportunities to escape. His reach was wider, his stride longer and his anticipation of her movements was a hunter's. He allowed her the freedom of thinking she was clever. Minny blinked in approval.

By the time he captured her, she was almost helpless with laughter and squeals, and breathless with her manipulations. She backed into a corner, crowding herself into it, her arms crossed over her chest. How interesting, she was so instinctively a woman at bay.

But she was laughing. She wasn't afraid. Her fingers on both hands were crossed and she said, "King's X! Time out! I have to catch my breath!"

"That's not one of the rules. Not in this game."

"Oh, yes!" She was positive. "Right down there at the bottom, it says: And if Georgia Brown Baines runs out of breath, she gets a King's X time-out. Hadn't you noticed that before you signed it?"

Formidably, he braced a hand on each wall holding her in the corner, blocking any escape. He smiled, his yellow eyes cauldrons of bronze and gold fire. "Catch your breath."

And she caught it, to hold it. He was intimidating, thrilling. Standing there, he appeared bigger than the room. Her game of teasing, which he'd played so willingly, had led to something else. No, she had intended it to lead to her capture by him. But he was a little overwhelming. And for the first time, she truly felt like a captive. Of Luke's.

He had her heart.

He was watching her intently. She leaned forward, and without touching him, she kissed his mouth very softly in surrender. He allowed that, kissing her back. He kept his hands on the wall and their bodies didn't touch. It was very erotic.

It was what he'd done to her at first—only kissing, not touching—and he had driven her crazy with desire. But tonight he wouldn't have to go to bed to sigh and twist with unslaked need, as she had done. He would go to sleep sated from her body.

And so would she sleep relaxed, replete.

Their play had filmed their bodies, concentrated their attentions sharply on each other and teased their need. It had been fun. They had both enjoyed it. But now the teasing was over. Now, their play would be of another kind.

Knowing that, she began it enticingly. She touched her tongue to his lips in a tiny Minny lick. He allowed that, too, and his tongue welcomed hers. His eyes on her were avid; his body trembled a little.

Since he was braced on his hands, his lower body was slanted away from her and she couldn't easily press herself to him. She put her hands up to his head to hold it gently, and openmouthed, she breathed along his cheek to his ear, before she tilted her head to brush her lips along his throat. He shivered.

Her panting breath turned into something more breathless. Their laughter was gone. He didn't adjust his height to hers so, in order to put her arms up around his shoulders, she had to go up on tiptoe, almost hanging from him, and he carried her weight easily as he allowed that, too.

She began to writhe, for she wanted to be against him. She frowned and made little discontented noises as she tried. He didn't move. She released his shoulders and gave him a hair-raising kiss, touching only his lips. He swallowed noisily and breathed through his mouth.

She looked into his eyes, with hers almost screened by her heavy lids. She smiled slowly and licked her lower lip, deliberately leaving it damp from her tongue. Still watching him, she lifted his T-shirt and bunched it up under his armpits—since he was acting as if his hands were glued to the wall. She gave him another soft smile.

She put her head down along his chest and closed her eyes as she explored it with her fingers and tongue. He gasped and twitched and his breath was hot in her hair. She ran a nail around his male nipple, then tried to suckle it. She licked and nibbled, and he shuddered. But he left his hands against the wall.

She examined his navel quite minutely and contemplated the barrier of his shorts. She looked up into the molten lava of his eyes and wrinkled her brow as if puzzled how to continue, but he didn't take his hands from the wall.

She walked around him as if trying to solve the puzzle, then "found" the button and "discovered" the zipper. She found the zipper fascinating, and had to run it up and down several times to see how it worked. That became very difficult very quickly.

His breath labored and he watched her avidly. Unmoving.

She ran the zipper down and began to ease his shorts off his hips. He had to move a little then, to help her. But he kept his hands in place.

Busily she pulled his shorts down his hairy legs and off over his bare feet. He stood there naked except for the T-shirt bunched up under his armpits, and his hands were still on the wall as he faced the corner.

She investigated him as if it was he who was her captive. How easily they had fallen into this new game. As she knelt there on the floor before him, she ran her hands up his hairy legs, relishing the difference of his texture. She felt his calf muscles, which were as hard as iron.

She moved behind him and stood as her hands caressed his back down to hard male buttocks. And she very sneakily slid a hand down between his legs and about lifted him off the floor. He made a hoarse sound; she laughed a low, sexy chuckle.

Back in her corner, she very, very slowly took off her own clothes. He watched. His yellow-brown eyes were almost red with his fires. She smiled as she stood there naked. And he held his position.

She moved around him, like a snake, clinging to him, kissing him, brushing her nakedness against his. And she found his breaking point. His primitive cry was rough, and she laughed.

He snatched her up and carried her over his shoulder into the bedroom to flip her over onto the bed. She bounced, laughing silkily.

He couldn't wait for her. She'd taunted him too far. He had to have her. And when he found her feminine lure hot and damp, he did just that. Quick, hard and wild, he took her to completion.

He sank down on her with murmurs of satisfaction—almost purrs of relished contentment. And her laugh was throaty, pleased she'd given him such pleasure.

As they settled into each other's arms that August night Luke set his watch alarm, and they drifted into sleep as they wanted to, with their well-used naked bodies touching, their arms lax in their embrace, their breaths mingling.

It was Minny who alerted them. She growled. She jumped up on Luke's chest. She hissed and growled. He said, "Huh?"

"Something's wrong," Georgia knew that instantly. "Luke, something's wrong."

"Sh-h-h-h," he whispered. "Don't you move an inch. Stay right there." He slid from the bed and was gone in the dark.

Minny went with him.

That left Georgia, naked, sitting up in a pitch-dark room, holding a sheet against her chest, straining her ears and hearing nothing.

The balcony lights went on, there was a roaring snarl from Luke and the sound of the sliding door, another roar, then a spitting hiss from Minny.

Georgia went to the bedroom door and peeked out. Luke was striding from the living room to the study. He punched the buttons on the phone with their resulting squeak, and snapped one word into the phone before he dropped it back down. Then he called the complex security, which rang and rang and rang.

Minny came in off the balcony walking arrogantly with her tail high. She went in and jumped up on

Luke's desk, and he put his big hand on her head.
"Good girl."

"What happened?" Georgia questioned.

"Someone was on the balcony. He jumped into the
bush below and ran. Our security saw him. They're
chasing him."

"A burglar?"

"Maybe." Luke looked at her. "Maybe only that."

And Georgia was finally convinced someone was
making some effort to steal her from Luke. Finally all
the things they'd warned her about became real. She
could be captured by a stranger. Someone who might
not be as kind as Luke and Mac. And she was scared.

There was finally a call. The burglar had gotten
away. Luke was curt. Then he looked at Georgia, naked still, leaning against the computer table, and he
went to her.

He took her into his arms in a very possessive way,
and he kissed her rather roughly. Then he carried her
back to the bed and he took her. It was as if he was
reiterating his claim to her in the most primal manner
in which a man shows his possession of a woman. She
was his.

And she gave herself quickly for the same reason.
She was indeed his. As he separated from her and lay
back, she moved to him. He took her close and his kiss
was a brand.

After a time, she said, "I suppose you should catch
a mouse for Minny."

"I'm a rotten mouse-catcher. I might manage a
sliver of liver."

"Was it Herb?"

Luke looked at her, licked his lips and replied,
"Perhaps."

After such a physically strenuous day, Luke should have gone right to sleep. There was no chance of anyone else getting anywhere near the complex, much less all the way to his particular unit. There was security out there of some determined people.

In the darkness, Luke lay a hand on Georgia's hip and smiled wolfishly. He relished what had happened, all of it. With the threat to his woman, he'd gone out in the darkness and scared the hell out of some innocently intruding thief.

Luke recalled the man's shock. That'd teach the intruder to come sneaking into Luke Montana's territory. His territory. He subtly stretched the body Georgia had pleasured, as he rubbed his hairy chest, and he was pleased with himself.

He'd protected his woman. The thought had simply emerged. His woman? In this day and age?

It wasn't a grin which then bared his teeth.

Minny came up onto his chest with a small greeting mew, and Luke's big hand gently curled around the tiny body as she began to purr. "Good girl," he whispered the compliment to her for waking him in time. It was nice the cat liked him.

Lying close to Luke on that big bed, Georgia, too, was thoughtful. There had been danger. Not just Herb wanting to talk to her, but that he would be willing to go to such lengths to get to her? And stark-naked, Luke had gone out to confront them! She'd heard his snarl. It had lifted the soft hairs on her spine. She'd thought the snarl had been from the invader. That primitive sound had been made by Luke!

Even as it thrilled her that he would defend her so rashly, it scared her a little, too. The power of him!

The maleness. It was far beyond what she expected from a man.

She carefully moved her well-loved body, wondering what was in store for her. Gradually she relaxed and almost slept, when she jerked awake. Luke's snore was barely interrupted as he patted her hip. She lay awake, then again slept, wakening, to sleep again.

In the morning, she and Luke bathed and dressed. It was the ninth day. Georgia dressed in a denim skirt with a light blue sleeveless blouse. She'd washed her hair and swirled it onto the top of her head.

The couple were comfortably silent as they changed the sheets. They had to wash them one at a time because his washer was quite small and the king-size sheets too big.

He stood looking down at her, his face solemn. "Are you all right?"

She smiled then, "Oh, yes."

He took her into his arms and kissed her. It was exquisitely gentle. Different from any kiss he'd given her. She sighed, leaned against him and kissed him back.

"Did you sleep all right?"

"With you and Minny on guard—and both of you sleeping solidly—I slept like a log." The dark shadows under her eyes showed that wasn't true.

"You're safe here. I've promised you that."

She touched his face. "What would you like for breakfast?"

"You."

She shook her head. "That wouldn't satisfy your appetite." She meant in volume as food.

"You could work on it all day, and I'd help." Her cheeks pinked charmingly, and his eyes changed. "Kiss me again."

She did that quite willingly before they moved to the kitchen, where she had to figure out what she was doing there. He stood near her and distracted her entirely.

"Sit here," she told Luke, as she set his place on the drop-leaf table in the living room. "Then you can look out into the trees."

She fixed his breakfast and watched him eat. When he sat back replete, she said "Try this," as she spread some cream cheese and raspberry jam on a gingerbread cookie and held it for him.

Watching her eyes, he allowed her to feed him. She licked her lip as he did, and he kissed her.

It was only later, as they sat in the living room, that Georgia said, "I hadn't thought there was really any danger. This whole thing is so unbelievable."

"So are you. I've never been driven so wild as you did me last night."

"You are magnificent." Her smile was almost shy.

"I wish we'd met under other circumstances."

She misunderstood and grinned. "What's a nice girl like me doing in a place like this?"

He watched her soberly. "Something like that."

She glanced quickly at him. There had been something in his tone that was almost too serious.

But he said, "You've really wrung me out, woman."

She stretched leisurely and his eyes went down her body. She laughed and tousled his hair. "How could I possibly interest you by this time? I'm surprised you're not saying, 'Who needs a woman around?' " And she grinned at his expected reply.

Luke held her hand. His eyes were on her almost constantly. He didn't talk or tease or move away from her. He kept a hand on her and he watched her.

Georgia wasn't sure what he expected her to do. She had made love with him, and now he was different in yet another way. How strange men are. How complicated. He was almost acting as if she was his.

There were no words of love.

From the beginning, she had known it would only be an affair. Why did she now notice the lack of a declaration? His wasn't the possessiveness of a man for a beloved woman. It was as a captor for a captive. Property.

There was that other—unsettling feeling in her. There was the tone of his voice, when he'd said he wished he'd met her under other circumstances. Now this. As close as he was, there was almost a separation, that was all it could be called. Strange.

Since she had been confused by him, she had avoided looking at him. She looked at him now, and their eyes were guarded. She turned her head, uncertain, and he took her chin to hold it as he kissed her. But that was possession. He didn't kiss her to comfort her or reassure her.

And he held on to her as if she would flee if he let go. Or if he released her, someone might snatch her? The idea made her restless.

After breakfast when Mac arrived, he said, "Well, I hear you had a nibble!"

Luke made a disgusted sound.

Georgia said, "Nibble? That makes me sound like bait."

Mac grinned. "I always miss all the excitement. How did he get clear up on the balcony?"

"We were...watching the news." Georgia gave Minny an apologetic look. How could she say Minny wakened them?

"Did you get a look at him?" Mac asked Luke.

"No."

"You're losing your touch. Getting old. In your younger days, you'd have been over that rail and nailed him before he hit the ground. I think you ought to give up baking, Georgia. He's getting fat and sluggish."

"You missed Georgia's Oriental chicken, Mac. It was great." He smiled at Georgia. Then he told Mac, "If you behave, and make no more little snide remarks about my age and weight, you might be able to talk me out of one of the rest of the meringue cookies."

"Meringue?" Mac perked up.

"They are perfect."

"Would you like one?" Georgia asked Luke.

"That'd be great."

"I'll get you some."

Mac frowned at Georgia. "He's capable of walking all the way across the living room."

"He's been chasing burglars," Georgia said back over her shoulder.

"He didn't *catch* one."

Luke pried his muscular body up out of the chair, and Mac bragged about him for being able to do that. Luke showed them he could walk as far as the table. Mac made rude noises; but as much as he had scoffed at Georgia waiting on Luke, Mac allowed her to serve him, too.

Georgia put a plate of cookies and a cup of coffee in front of Luke and said, "Those are the best ones."

And as he smiled at her, she straightened and listened to what she'd said. It was just the way her mother told her father! She'd given Luke the best.

They ate as they discussed what would be done with the burglar, if he was ever caught. They talked about who it might have been. That was silly, because all three acted as if they knew who had been behind the attempt to get into the apartment.

Mac was a little impatient, because he couldn't seem to get Luke's complete attention. "Security followed the intruder all the way to Thirty-eighth Street, but lost him somewhere down by the fairgrounds. He was limping."

"He jumped off the balcony." Luke's grin was dangerous.

"I heard that. I can't understand why you let him get away?"

"He could have been diversionary."

"Well, yes, I suppose so."

Georgia rose and stretched, with an economy of movement. "This is the ninth day."

Both men looked at her.

She asked, "How's it going? You said a week to ten days. Tomorrow's the tenth."

"Now..." Luke said in a placating tone. "It's probably going to be several more days."

"My birthday is coming up in a couple of months and my parents will expect me home, you know."

"Just another few days," Luke said again.

Mac was silent for a minute, then he turned back to Luke. "Luke—"

Perhaps it was his tone, but Luke said, "Excuse us, Georgia? We'll just go into the study."

It was there that Mac said, "Parker said the guy was probably just an ordinary everyday run-of-the-mill burglar who has probably had the essence scared out of him and reformed him."

"Probably."

Mac scolded tersely, "You can't keep Georgia locked up much longer. You have to know that."

"A few more days."

Mac stood up and walked to the window. "We're getting rumors that Simon's bunch and Mary-Ellen's group are both as close as we are to something like the Molly Q."

"I didn't know they were that close."

"They must have better security."

"You know perfectly well that no one can beat Olivia with our own security." Luke asked, "How close are they?"

"From what we hear, they may already have it!"

"The only threat we could see was Herb."

"Not Olivia." Mac shook his head. "She watches everybody."

"If it should break, don't tell me in front of Georgia. Just tell me. I'll handle it from there."

"I hope to God you know what you're doing."

"Trust me."

"I can. I'm not Georgia."

"I'm not going to hurt her."

"If you make her unhappy, you'll have to convince me she's not hurt."

Although the sentence didn't make real sense, both men knew what Mac meant. His first loyalty was to Luke, but he was concerned for Georgia.

Eight

Mac moved to the study door, as he said, "I probably won't be by tomorrow unless it breaks. I worked last Sunday and if I try to do that again, Penny will have your ears."

With the residual dregs of last night's primitive man, Luke asked lazily, "Can't you control your woman?"

And with a modern man's adjustment to the status quo, Mac grinned and replied, "I find it's more fun if she thinks she's in control."

Then as Mac opened the study door, Luke said to him, "Remember, don't mention anything in front of Georgia—"

"Now, Luke—"

And Georgia asked, "Don't mention—what—in front of Georgia?"

They had left her down at the other end of the living room, but she was just coming from the bathroom and she had heard them both.

Mac said, "Uh—"

But Luke quickly covered Mac's word by saying smoothly, "It may be just a little longer than we'd planned. It might be two weeks."

Mac looked blank.

"Another five days?" And while her words sounded right, Luke saw that she almost smiled, and he was thrilled. She wanted to stay with him?

Mac stood there for a minute and looked at the two, then he sighed, went in and gathered up the paperwork off Luke's desk and said, "I'll see what can be done with this mess." And he left.

Luke turned his hand palm-up and Georgia went to him readily enough. He held her, just held her. He petted back her hair, kissed her forehead, ran his hand down her arm, tilted back her head to look into her eyes and hugged her. Then he smiled.

He said, "I think we have a free weekend. What would you like to do?"

"I've never done any hang gliding. I would like that very much, but I'm a bit afraid of heights. The idea of it appeals to me, but the actuality of it is a little scary."

"It's the closest thing to being a bird and it's great. You don't feel like a pedestrian. You feel you're a part of the whole and not just a speck plodding along, trapped on the earth's surface. It's exhilarating."

"You've done it."

"Back in my reckless days."

"You're past your reckless days?"

"Oh, yes." He smiled some more. "I'm about ready to settle down."

"If you're past your days of being reckless, how do you justify capturing an innocent bystander and holding her captive, for nine days now?"

"Anyone I know?"

"You're holding her in your arms."

"Are you an innocent bystander?" He was no longer smiling, and he'd made his eyes serious.

"What else?"

"You're the most beautiful woman in all the world. An alluring siren, who could charm the secrets from any man."

She grinned. "Could I?"

"Would you?"

In his arms, she folded hers on his chest and lay her chin on them in great thought.

"What are you thinking?" he asked her.

"I'm trying to figure out what I'd like to know."

"You don't know what to ask?"

She stretched her arms up, and his eyes went down to her chest as his arms tightened around her, drawing her closer. She teased, "Let's see. I suppose—being older—you must know more than I? Women don't interest me, although you are obviously an expert in that field—"

"No."

"And I suppose you know about cars, football, umm, and beer, if the contents of the refrigerator and your brief dissertation are any indication. None of those has any gripping interest to me. However, if you feel an irresistible need to expound on any of the above, go ahead. I am tolerant."

"So what interests you?"

"You amaze me."

"Why?"

"You are so unpredictable. You are such a complete man. You astound me. And you are so bullheaded and arbitrary—"

"I am not!"

"And so kind and gentle. And you are a magnificent lover."

"Really?"

"Umm. And you scared me to death, rushing out to investigate when Minny said there was trouble. And you snarled at that poor man."

"That . . . poor man?"

"You're supposed to lie still and pretend to be asleep when someone invades your house."

"Horsefeathers."

"*Horsefeathers?* Where did you find that word?"

"Penny forbids Mac to say anything vulgar. We have become quite inventive in expressing ourselves while keeping within her limitations. Mac, you see, says he picks up on words and repeats them automatically, so we all have to watch our mouths to save his neck with Penny."

"I like your friendship with Mac."

"He's one of the good ones."

"Will I ever get to meet Penny? I find I am extremely curious about her. What's she look like?"

"Of course, you'll meet Penny. When this is over, we'll live perfectly normal lives. We'll get to swim and see people and . . . Do you dance?"

He meant she was to stay? Or that they would still see each other? He wasn't just taking advantage of this remarkable situation to exercise his male needs?

"I dance quite adequately." She lifted her chin and gave him a smug look.

"I'll bet you dance like feather down. And you draw beautifully and jog gorgeously, and—"

"You haven't mentioned cooking."

"Your cheesecake is superb, your omelets must rival Julia Child's—"

"What about the popovers or the cucumber soup?"

"Well ... they need a little work."

"Why, Luke! How could you! You're *supposed* to say 'rather unusual.' Or 'quite interesting.' 'Need a little work!'" She snorted. "How rude!" She was disgusted with him.

"How about 'I've never seen anything like them'?"

She had to laugh, and so did he. Then he kissed her, sweet kisses.

"Want to go up on the roof?" he offered.

"Yes. But I'm not sure I can jog. I don't understand it, but my body feels tired, and as if it's gone though something remarkable."

"Really?" He looked down at her. "In what way?"

"I can hardly walk."

"Perhaps you need a good oil massage."

"I wouldn't dare."

"I wouldn't call in a crass stranger who might be rough and...unfeeling." It was a noble offer. "I'd do it."

"I'll just bet you would! I do appreciate the offer, which I know comes from the kindness of your heart without any ulterior motive, but I think I'll pass this time. Thanks, anyway."

"It would relax us both."

"You've already been 'relaxed' this morning. Are you taking extra vitamins?"

They went to the roof, taking Minny along, and leaving her to her own explorations, they walked the

perimeter...holding hands, talking, laughing and
flirting. The roof of that unit was half a block in
length, so their thirty casual circuits amounted to a fair
walk.

When they went back to the apartment, they left
Minny up there, for there were trees along the edge
which shaded the roof, allowing endless bird-watching
opportunities for the little cat.

In Luke's living room, Georgia lolled on the sofa
and entertained herself with another kind of watching. She watched Luke lift weights. He said, "You
should lift some of the light ones for muscle tone."

She wasn't interested. She got her sketchbook and
drew him.

"Do I have to hold still?" he asked.

"No. At art school we learned to draw moving
things. All of one afternoon, we drew puppies in a
large wire cage. We had been accustomed to drawing
static things. Still lifes, unmoving models, and we were
boggled to try to draw the puppies who wouldn't hold
still.

"Our instructor said, 'Watch. This is the way you
draw children. You do sketches all over the page of
different viewpoints. As the figure moves, you work
on the sketch the move matches. As it changes, you
change to another sketch.'

"He explained that people and animals move in
patterns. You will find each pose touched on many
times. Then you will know your subject from *any* an-
gle, and from your sketches you can draw your finished pose. It was amazing to watch that. He was
right. It was fascinating."

"I haven't seen you draw since you've been here."

"I've done some. Pencil."

Interested, he said, "Let me see."

"They're nothing. Just roughs."

"Won't you show me?"

She blushed as she peeked through pages, and that alerted him. He watched her and saw that she selected specific pages to show him sketches of Minny. He reached for the pad, but she held it and gave him only brief glimpses. What was she hiding? Had she opened the folder of the Molly Q, after all?

He didn't push to see what was in the book then. He could have, but he didn't. He would watch where she put the pad. And he was careful to appear indifferent.

"I suppose you've had a lot of opportunity to sketch Minny. You draw her extremely well. She's a beautiful cat and you have caught her beautifully."

That pleased Georgia.

He watched her as she flipped quite a chunk of pages back to the place she was drawing him exercising. She studied him minutely. That she would look at him that way made him self-conscious. Conscious of himself. Aware of his body. That he was a male being closely studied by a female.

Naturally that made him more aware of her body and that she was a female and a willing one, at that. "You really ought to lift weights. Since we have the time, I could get you started. Stand up."

She put aside her pad and pencil and stood before him.

"This movement," he instructed, "will tone these muscles." He traced the line of muscles. "And this one does all these." He bent her and traced all those that simple movement would affect.

One thing led to another, and he relaxed them both.

* * *

They retrieved Minny from the roof, and bird-watching can be exhausting, so the little cat curled by the glass sliding door and napped. The lovers fixed a lazy lunch, and although they hadn't done any bird-watching, they, too, napped.

Georgia was very tired and had slept poorly the night before, so her sleep was deep and dreamless. He watched her for a long time, then eased from the bed and went naked into the living room to sit on his heels down by her box of books, and he sneaked out her sketchbook.

He held it in his hands, as if reluctant to witness what might be inside. Then he opened it and slowly went through the pages.

There were sketches and drawings of many things. People, Minny, a droll scruffy dog, but nothing about the Molly Q. However, there was a whole series of Luke Montana.

Luke went through those very slowly and his eyes glowed and his lips held a smug smile. They were fantasy and they were Luke as the hero—and a familiar female in the role as rescued but mostly captive maiden.

There were clinches that steamed on the page and filled him with delight, for obviously she craved him. There were embraces that lifted his hair and sent a tickle down his sated body. And the renderings were beautiful. She was very skilled.

Then just before the sketches of him exercising, there was a page filled with babies...

She had said she could no longer face children. Yet here were sketches of babies. A page of them. And he thought how carefully she must know children, to draw them so well. How much she loved them.

He returned the pad to its precise place, and he went back to her bed. He lay down beside her and took her into his arms.

"What's wrong?" she asked fighting toward consciousness.

"Absolutely nothing." His deep voice purred against her temple. "Everything is just right. Go to sleep."

She did. He didn't. He held her and he smiled.

For supper they had browned hamburger with onions, to which she added fresh chopped spinach with raw beaten eggs. It was done as soon as the spinach wilted, so it was quickly done. She served it with the melon salad and more of her bread dough baked in rolls. He ate a staggering amount and relished it all. He made appreciating sounds as he ate, and he charmed her.

Then Luke chose videotapes of Mac playing football. He didn't mention that one wide receiver was Luke Montana. She finally read it on his jersey and exclaimed, "It's *you!*"

"Uh . . . yeah. But watch Mac throw this one! He's a genius. See? I'm not even looking. See me stumble? He *compensates* for it."

"Go back! Were they all you? Let me see again. I've heard of a Montana who plays football, is that you?"

"No, he's another football player. He's good. A little younger. No kin."

"Go back and let me see."

She got very excited. She screeched when he was creamed. She gave all his catches "body English," helping him do something done long past and finished. When he got up from under a peeled-back pile

of bodies—and limped—she agonized. She gasped
when he leapt impossibly to catch a totally impossible
ball. She twitched with the shoe-top ones, and she
clutched at him.

"I had no idea you were a football fan." He was
amazed.

"I'm not. It's a terrible game. People could get
hurt!"

"Would you like to watch the Super Bowl? I have
it."

"Are you in it?"

"No, it's this year's."

"No."

"It was a great game! The teams were so evenly
matched, it was a real pro game. The blocking was remarkable, neither quarterback was sacked. Brilliant."

"Who won?"

"You discourage me a little, asking that. It makes
me suspect you're not a true fan. The score was three
to nothing. A field goal kicked from the *forty-nine-
yard line.*"

"Obviously that's impressive?"

"Well, it is a feat."

She lifted her brows minutely. "It's a feat done with
feet."

"You're not one of those?" He shook his head to
encourage a denial. "You don't like wordplay."

"Do I look like one of those?"

"No, you look like a nice, clean woman who is
normal and who could take up an avid interest in pro
football."

"Looks can be deceiving."

"No chance at all?"

"None."

"Well, we do share other interests." He smiled.

"Not anymore today. What other films do you have?"

"I have some promo tapes."

"Fascinating." Her tone was not sincere.

He frowned. "They're very good!"

"What else?"

"More football."

"Films? Movies?"

"Sorry."

"Not even the story of Knute Rockne?"

"You know about him? That's a start! What else do you know about football?"

She countered. "What do you know about art?"

"Not a whole lot. My exposure has been limited mostly to the walls of men's rest rooms."

"Shocking."

He demurred. "Informative folk art."

She laughed.

"What would you like to do for entertainment this evening? We've a long, uninterrupted evening ahead of us. I know! I'll teach you wrestling holds."

But they played backgammon. And they argued. And they decided what the President should do about the Middle East, and they worked on a plan to refor-est the world.

They slept in each other's arms and all the rest of the bed was empty. Three or four other people could have slept there, too. It was really too much room just for Minny.

And it was lovely to awaken and to lie close and to kiss. His breath was sweet and his kisses delicious. They bathed together, and in the kitchen they bumped against each other fixing a picnic breakfast. They grinned a lot. They were alone.

Their weekend was a dream. They laughed and talked. They took their picnic to the roof, where they lay in the early sun and strolled about as they exchanged ideas, opinions and prejudices. They watched Minny watch the birds. And he wanted to make love there.

"On the roof? This is a scandal!"

"It isn't a roof." He frowned in scoffing. "It's a mountaintop!"

"How foolish of me. It's the sun. Only mad dogs and Englishmen go out in the midday sun. I'm a bit English. I suppose that's why I'm out here on a roof, pretending it's a mountaintop and allowing a strange man to seduce me?"

"Are you allowing it?"

He had all her clothes off, she was flat on her back on the blanket, which didn't quite pad the gravel enough, and he was doing all sorts of provocative things to her body.

"No," she replied, "I'm not allowing it. I'm only enduring."

What a foolish thing to say to a man like Luke. He had to prove she was mistaken. He moved back from her and watched her with a particularly sly smile, then he went to work on her.

There is nothing quite like a man who has a ready supply of loving at hand, who isn't too needful and wants to entice a woman. Make her squirm and need. Make her wild.

Since he enjoyed women and treasured them, he was particularly skilled. It didn't take him long. But in teasing her, he'd become hotly aroused himself, and she responded so thrillingly that he continued her enticement far beyond his original goal.

From the picnic basket, he took a bottle of oil and gave her his oil massage. And with the heat of the August day, the oil became filmed with sweat and she was very slippery. Soon, so was he. To rub a hand down her body was mesmerizing to his hand and to his eyes. To watch the glistening movement of her breasts under his hands made his body ache. His mouth opened to aid his breathing as she slowly writhed almost like a supine belly dancer as, in her desire, she moved her body and slowly shifted her arms and legs.

Her hair became sweaty and oily, and she looked like a mermaid cast up from some magical sea. And he made love to her. Her little squeaks and gasps drove him wild.

He turned her, knelt as he looked down at her, rubbed his hands up from her ankles, and he eased down and filled her. She gasped. He waited. She moaned. He moved. She pressed up, tilting her hips against him. And he began that long, beautiful flight.

It was a while before she commented, "I'll never get the oil out of my hair."

"You look exotic. Like a mermaid."

"And you're a shipwrecked sailor?"

"I think I drowned and went to sailor's heaven. Davy Jones's locker?"

"This entire time has been astonishing."

"Stay with me." He surprised himself a little. He'd meant to be a little more casual about it.

"Live with you?"

"You wouldn't have to take your pictures down. They look very nice on my walls. And you look even better in my house."

"What would I tell my parents?" she asked logically. "They are very old-fashioned."

"Tell them . . . Tell them you have an unusually friendly apartment mate. I want you to stay with me."

She shook her head. "It's only propinquity. If you saw me under ordinary circumstances, you'd look right past me."

"No." He was sure.

"I'm not beautiful."

He could not control a blurting laugh of disbelief, but he straightened his face as well as he could. He leaned away and looked at her lying there in the sunlight, shiny with oil, her body soft and lax and well-loved. "You're not bad." He grinned. Then he teased, "And that one hundred thousand you're getting from us *is* something to consider."

"When will you know about the Molly Q? When will I be free?"

He frowned. "Do you want to leave?"

"To ask me to stay, now, is meaningless. I am your prisoner. I have to stay."

Later, while she was showering, Mac called Luke, and told him the whole Molly Q experiment was up for grabs, for it had been confirmed that three other companies had just about the same thing. Luke said, "Don't tell Georgia."

"Luke, you have to let her go."

"Don't worry about a thing. I'll take care of her."

"You could get into one hell of a lot of trouble."

"I can't let her go."

"You're not thinking about this clearly. At least tell her she's in no danger. Let her know you trust her. Give her some space. You underestimate yourself, Luke, and how women react to you."

Luke didn't reply, and Mac urged. "You've never before been this way about a woman. You will overwhelm her. And you're a workaholic. You know that. Nothing comes before that company of yours. You shouldn't do this to her. You'll give her all this time, and she'll think this is the way her life will go, and then you'll get enough sex to last through the day, and you'll go off and she won't see you again until bedtime. Be honest with her, Luke. Tell her."

"I'll think about it seriously. But not today. Maybe tomorrow."

"Don't put it off."

"You don't understand."

"Luke, the other companies are making oblique inquiries about pooling our research. You need to decide."

"You handle it."

There was a hesitation, then Mac's voice brightened with excitement. "You'd let me?"

It was Luke's turn to pause, then he grinned and said, "I trust you. You know as much as I do. You're on top of all the aspects. Let me know how it works out."

"Can I bring Mike and George in on this? We need to give them more responsibility."

"You're right. Do it. Good luck."

"My God! This is great! Luke, there's hope for you, yet! Good luck, yourself. She's almost as precious as Penny. Be careful. Tell her. Don't louse up."

But Luke didn't tell Georgia she was free, that he had not even the flimsiest excuse to continue her captivity.

She fixed him a pork crown roast with yams, corn on the cob, sauerkraut of white and red cabbage, applesauce and more of her rolls. The rolls came out quite evenly matched in size. Her loaves were still mismatched.

She sketched him as he lifted his weights, and she teased him about his bulging muscles and made him laugh. He chased her as she fled, and she became better at dodging him and escaping. He even had to work a little before he caught her. He outlawed King's *X*.

They could argue heatedly over things without becoming angry or personal. Luke never blamed her for anything. It was never she who was wrong, it was her information. It was never she who had failed. She wasn't practiced. And he laughed.

He laughed, he enjoyed, he was tender, he teased, he was interested in so many things. He was curious, he could be amazed, he called her attention to things and shared. He was a whole man. He was his own man. He controlled his own life. And he loved it.

It was that Sunday that she realized she was free. Her self-imposed guilt over Phillip's tragically shortened life was gone.

It was as her parents had told her all along: Phillip was responsible for himself. We all are guaranteed only the *pursuit* of happiness. And it was as Luke had said: If your goals are beyond your reach, shorten your goals.

At last, Georgia could be sad for Phillip without being crippled by him. She was free.

Free?

"This is the tenth day," she mentioned to Luke.

"It's great having you here."

She laughed. "You added an extra word. You should have just said, 'It's great having you.'"

"Do you feel you've . . . been had?"

"Sex, a cook, a laundress. I will have earned the ten thousand per day."

"You are altering the wordage in the contract. It wasn't ten thousand per day, it was a flat one hundred thousand."

"Ten per day." She scrubbed out the baking pan before she put it in the dishwasher. The dishwasher was like any cleaning device, it was choosy about what it actually cleaned.

He mentioned, "At ten thousand per day, if your confinement went on for two months, you would own a fair portion of the company."

With a magnanimous gesture, she conceded: "I would allow you and Mac to continue running it, but I would be an active stockholder and supervise."

"When you dictated your demands, would you hold me on your lap?"

"And squash my thighs?" she gasped. "No, I'd use the couch and convince you that way."

"I have noticed a shocking preoccupation in you for sex. You pester me without pause—"

She lifted her soapy hands and frowned at them. "Have you paws been neglecting that boy?"

He put a hand to his head and groaned. Then he gave her a stern look. ''I have heard that the way to cure someone of a mania is to grant them an excess of their desire.'' He smiled.

''You are feeling used?'' A while ago, it had been his question. She smiled a little. ''You want to cure me? And you have just the method? Excessive sex?''

''We could only try.''

''I like things the way they are.''

''You are rejecting excessive sex?''

She leaned forward, allowing her scoop-neck blouse to dip invitingly and she said with soft lips, ''I'm rejecting being cured.''

He laughed and hugged her and walked her into the living room, where there was more room, and he swung her around and then hugged her some more.

They lolled through the time, that Sunday, anticipating going to bed together, to sleep again in each other's arms. Sharing that intimacy.

Then they would awaken within reach. To smile and start the day with the other so close. To kiss. To rise and stretch and yawn. To bathe together.

''I'm getting very good at giving women baths.''

''You're not to open a shop for bathing ladies.''

''You'd be jealous?'' That delighted him.

''It wouldn't be kind for you to tease another woman and get her all excited, because you would not be able to make love to her.''

''You'd object and stop me.''

''You'd go to work too tired to try.''

His head went back to laugh and he almost drowned in the sudsy water.

They read all the Sunday papers and discussed the news. They lay on their stomachs on the floor, and had to move Minny in order to read the comics. It was a lovely, lazy day.

Nine

They ate and then settled in to watch the football exhibition game. Luke said, "This is great! I haven't been able to just sit and watch in so long. I've been so involved—but you know about that."

Georgia said very seriously, "You have to realize, by now, that I know nothing about your business."

He gave her a smile. "It's electronics. We make computer—"

"Don't tell me!"

He was surprised. "Why not?"

"If that Herb should get to me."

"Oh." And Luke was made aware that she might not accept the fact that she had been fooled and there had been no basis for her captivity.

Georgia indicated the TV. "I'm not sure I can watch this mayhem."

Luke was diverted from his uncertainty. He'd figure out later what he should do. He replied, "Not mayhem, sport! It's a skill. Like your art. We have to talk about your awesome ability to draw. There has to be a way for you to make your living as an artist."

"Yes. But very few artists can make a living on their art alone. A book has a lot of copies, a product such as your company makes, has a wide market, a song can be sung forever, but an artist makes only one original."

"There are other ways. Box designs, book covers, that kind of art."

"And an excess of artists."

"You are exceptional." He kissed her temple, moved the bowl of popcorn and hugged her close to him. "You need me."

She was very contented. She smiled over the popcorn. He'd said, "Let's watch the *football* game!" as if that would be a treat for her. Then he added his coup: "I'll make my popcorn!" He asked suddenly, "Do you read lips?"

She shook her head. "Sorry."

"Good. The guys don't speak very nicely on the field."

"They...cuss?"

"Vulgarly."

"How shocking!"

So as the game progressed and he laughed when there wasn't anything to laugh about, she would ask, "What'd he say?" But Luke would only shake his head and cover her eyes with his hand.

Curled against him on the couch, the sounds of the game fading, she was almost asleep when his parents called. They were coming by to leave their dog. They were going to Lake Michigan for a cruise with some friends on their boat.

"Their…dog? What about Minny?" She asked that as they hurriedly carried her boxes into his study and closed the door on the chaos.

"We'll think of something. It's a very nice dog."

His parents were attractive people, tall and lean. His father's shoulders were wide, but his feminine mother was also built like an athlete. They were a little startled to see Georgia. That was a plus, for it meant a woman in Luke's apartment was not something they expected. They were pleasant, and curbed their curiosity.

The dog was something completely unexpected. For a family like the Montanas, with Luke's apartment, his clothes and car, and his parents' obvious life-style, the dog would have to be a registered canine. It was a mutt. And that was his name.

He was a perfect mutt, not too big, with gray, white and black rather long hair that peaked and looked windblown. He had button eyes.

He was alert, friendly, and he spotted Minny immediately, but he didn't do anything. He was used to cats? Minny watched from the top of the television, and he kept an interested, friendly eye on her.

Luke's mother almost immediately exclaimed, "The pictures! Marvelous!" She had a hard time being distracted from them. But she did look around and add: "The whole place looks better. It looks as if someone is going to live here."

While his Dad said, "Too bad about the Molly Q."

His mother said bracingly, "It was an interesting try."

"The Molly Q?" Georgia inquired carefully.

Luke cleared his throat, to give himself time to think of something to say.

"Sunk," his father said. Then, as if realizing Georgia might not know what they were talking about, he explained, "An experiment at the electronics company."

So the Molly Q hadn't worked? It had "sunk." Obviously other people thought the title sounded like a boat and not something mysterious that had an electronic application.

"The Molly Q?" she repeated as she looked at Luke.

"Uh . . ." he said brilliantly.

"When did that happen?" she inquired with a little too much polite interest.

"There were rumors on Thursday." His father studied his speechless son with thoughtfully narrowed eyes.

They hadn't even had time to sit down, so all four were standing there, with Mutt keeping an eye on Minny and Minny never taking her stare from the dog.

"Last Thursday?" Georgia's query about the exact day was marked.

Luke hastened to explain, negating Thursday. "Nothing was solid then. Only rumors."

His father tried to help. "That's right. It wasn't sure until yesterday."

"Last night?" Georgia turned polite eyes to Luke's father.

"In the morning?" Luke's father was a little uncertain and looked at Luke for guidance.

"I see." Georgia looked back at Luke. "I suppose it slipped your mind?"

"I didn't mention it?"

He knew good and well he hadn't, and it made her furious! She turned her calm face back to his parents and said, "I've been held here for almost two weeks."

"What do you mean?" his mother asked slowly.

"I've been held here against my will."

And his mother said to her son, "Now, what?"

To distract his mother, Luke told her, "She's learning to cook."

"Don't you cook, Georgia?"

Georgia didn't reply, but said to Luke, "It's exceedingly interesting and excessively *telling* that you have a mother who comes here, finds you've imprisoned a woman and she doesn't say, 'How shocking!' She says, 'Now, what.' That says a lot about you, Luke Montana."

His mother's head went up, his father looked at Luke, and Luke laughed. A genuine, amused, impulsive laugh. It made his father smile.

It made Georgia madder. She smiled sweetly and said a sugar-coated, "I know you'll want to tell them—about us. I'll just slip into your room and wait."

His parents exchanged a look, but Luke laughed again, coughing to conceal it, but he did that poorly. He said, "She's mad at me right now; don't pay any attention to her."

His mother raised her eyebrows a little, because she hadn't realized her son was that stupid about women, and his father flinched over his son's gaffe.

Georgia scooped Minny off the TV, swept into the bedroom and slammed the door. Minny was annoyed and asked to go back immediately. Georgia locked the door, and Minny put her ears back.

Georgia stormed around the room, mentally arguing with Luke and flinging her arms out in dramatic gestures. She was furious.

There was the bed. There, last night, Luke had climbed in with her, knowing there was no reason at all for holding her any longer. He'd slept with her and held her. And she hadn't known she was free to leave. How dared he?

Before she had marshaled a perfectly stunning script to sear his ears, the key turned in the bedroom-door lock and Luke entered, followed by the dog.

How tacky of him not to knock and ask permission to enter! It was a potentially explosive situation. A furious woman, an irritated cat, an unknowing man and a friendly dog who apparently had never been warned that, like some people, dogs and cats do not mix.

Luke said, "I didn't want you to leave."

Now *what* was she supposed to say to that? How could she be angry with a man who said the perfect thing at just the right time?

She turned toward him, but her arms were still crossed over her chest. She looked at him coldly.

He didn't smile or move. He just stood there, very serious. He watched her. And he didn't say anything more.

The dog had sat down, with his head tilted back, in order to look from one adult to the other. Then Minny hissed gently to attract his attention. The dog stood up willingly and trotted over toward the cat.

That did distract both adults, who began to move at the same time to intervene, but Minny solved the initial confrontation by jumping easily up onto the chest of drawers, to lean over the edge and look down at the friendly dog.

Since the tension had been zapped by the animals, Georgia turned to Luke and asked, "Why didn't you tell me?"

He moved his hands out in a seemingly helpless gesture and said again, "I didn't want you to leave me."

"You could have given me the choice."

"That's what Mac said."

"You discussed me with Mac?"

"Endlessly."

How could such a man manage to look vulnerable? "You are arbitrary," she accused him.

"How can you say that?"

"If you're not, what am I doing here and why is my car no longer pink?"

"You want it pink?" He couldn't believe that.

"No, but you should have asked me if I wanted it painted."

"I did! You said dark green."

"Yes. Well."

"Don't worry. I'm flexible. We can arbitrate anything."

She considered that. Then she asked, "Your parents left?"

"They said they'd see you next week. Mother says she loves your pictures, and the needlepoint pillows are exquisite, and she wants to know if you paint on canvases."

"Didn't they mention anything to you about keeping me here all this time? Doing God only knows what all to me?"

"My Dad said not to let you get away." He never took his eyes off her, and he was very tense.

"I'm sorry about the Molly Q."

He went to her slowly then, took her hand in both of his to lift it and kiss her fingers. He said, "Two other companies have almost the same thing. We can't make the killing, after all. You won't get the hundred thousand. We will still make a bundle on this, especially if Mac can get them to pool their findings and add them to ours."

He pushed out his lower lip as he narrowed his eyes and speculated, "You might get ten thousand." Then he said, "The good thing about all this is that Herb's company isn't one of the other two. He's out of it entirely." And he laughed a really dirty laugh.

"Only ten thousand?"

"That's not bad for ten days' sitting around, doing nothing."

"You probably kept me from landing the position of the century!"

His very deep voice said, "I know of a couple of positions you could take."

"A position which would have paid sixty thousand a year!" she continued.

"Herb fired you?" He nudged it.

"Herb? How could he fire me when I don't even know him?"

He had known, with the first security check, that she had never known Herb. But he found it droll to continue the game. "You can't count on Herb," Luke advised her. "He would fire you without turning a hair. That'd be just his style." He looked at his watch. "Come on. We can still see the rest of the game." He turned and tugged her along back into the living room.

Just like that, their confrontation was over? He had no excuses or apologies? He simply said he hadn't wanted her to leave, and that took care of everything? Apparently.

She lagged against his towing her along and she said, "I'm tired of having this . . . Herb shoved in my face."

"Me, too." He gave her a quick kiss. "Let's not talk about Herb."

"I'm not the one who talks about him, at all. It's . . ."

"And you needn't." He thought that was hilarious advice, since she didn't know Herb, but he was anxious to see the game and turned on the TV. He came back and sat her down next to him as the roar of the crowd gathered sound. Luke's concentration was on the screen as he said, "We'll forget Herb. He's out of your life from here on out. Okay?"

"He was never *in* my life!"

"That's a good attitude."

"Luke!"

"In just a minute, honey. Watch."

There was no opportunity to bring up the Molly Q again while the game was on, and even Georgia watched the beer commercials. After the game, it was suppertime. The cat and dog were playing tag, and the whole Herb thing didn't seem to matter any longer. That was weird.

They took Mutt out for a walk, and Georgia was amazed how important it was to be outside. Being on the roof had helped, but to actually walk on the ground! She was exuberant! And that made her situation and his arbitrary decisions about her freedom less urgent. She was free. Freer.

When they went to bed that night, Luke held her deliciously and he told her, "You need me."

"I've never known making love could be this way."

"You've never been like this with any other man?"

"I was a virgin when I married, and there's been no one else."

"Right."

"Luke..."

But he'd begun his magic. He had begun to make her respond. She lost track of what she had been saying and forgot the need to make him understand as the urgency of love took over.

He was so careful, that his touches were thrilling. He was such a diligent lover. He knew exactly what she needed, and saw to it she had all she wanted. And all he wanted.

His humor was especially good. His deep, chuckling laugh. His teasing. He was a special man. And he had been willing to take such a risk so that she would stay with him. She smiled and moved and pleasured him in turn.

She would forgive him. She would understand how much he'd wanted her. And that he wasn't too outrageous in keeping her with him, because of the risk to the Molly Q.

There was so much they shared in their opinions, there was so much she liked about him. He was so easy to get along with, and he was very kind to other people. Look how much Minny loved him. And Mac. And Georgia Brown Baines. She loved him, too, and she responded to his loving with all her being.

But when he finally could withdraw from her, when his breathing had steadied and he again had the strength, he patted her hip and asked, with teasing smugness, "Was Herb ever that good?"

She was still in shock the next morning. She hadn't slept at all. She lay awake and thought about Luke, and she decided she had to leave. He had never believed her.

He had had time to know her, to see what sort of woman she was, but he didn't trust her.

How could she stay with a man who didn't trust her word? If she hadn't been able to convince him in those ten days, could she ever?

She had lived for over a year with a discontented man. She would never again force herself to adjust to strange behavior. Luke's first wife had betrayed him, and apparently he couldn't give Georgia his trust. How would her life go, if she lived with Luke and he didn't trust her? It would be hell.

It would be hell without him, but it would be worse to live with him and have him doubt her. And he meant for her only to live with him. He said nothing about love or commitment, only of staying together.

When it came right down to it, she realized that she was the only one who could protect herself. She had her own pride and sense of worth. He had had ample opportunity to know her, to make love with her, to see what sort of woman she would be to live around, and he *still* didn't trust her.

She would go home where she could lick her wounds and heal. She had recovered from the devastation of Phillip. She would eventually recover from Luke. She probably would. How foolish she had been. She knew she would never again become involved with any man. It was too rough.

In the early morning's light, Luke awakened and stretched, then he turned and smiled his unfair smile at her. "Good morning, beautiful."

She was lying on her side, watching him, filling her eyes with him. How did the lines go from *Romeo and Juliet?* "Eyes, look your last! Arms, take your last embrace!" How could she leave him?

"Are you pensive? Chinese for breakfast?" He thought that was very funny.

How could he be so unaware he'd dealt her such a killing blow?

He raised up over her and turned her on her back. He kissed her with his unfair mouth, and gently rubbed his morning's whiskers along her face and throat...then down over her breasts. She was still naked from his lovemaking the night before, so nothing impeded him as he took advantage of her.

She didn't object. She told all her cells to be aware. This was the last time they would ever have the opportunity to know what it was like. They should absorb the feelings, so that she could remember how it had been.

And when he was finished, he lifted his head and looked down at her, and he kissed her very gently. "You're in a very strange mood—"

But the phone rang. It was plugged into the bedroom jack, so Luke still watched her as he groped for the phone. He held her gaze while he lay, still coupled to her, as he said, "Yes?"

He listened, then he said, "All right," and he put the phone back on its cradle.

He kissed her as he eased from her, and he said, "I'm going to the office today. That was Mac." He kissed her again. "The other companies are sending representatives to *us* to chat about the ramifications of their competition with our Molly Q.

"It is almost certain that since they are so interested in coming to us, we have more on this than they and they are petitioners. We can negotiate." He gave a wolfish smile she'd never seen.

"Will you have enough to keep you busy until I get home? Will you miss me?" He smiled quite smugly confident of her reply.

She gave it: "Yes. I'll miss you terribly."

He showered, and she lay in bed, feeling everything acutely. He came in and dressed as she watched, and he regarded her thoughtfully. "You'll be okay."

"Yes."

"Being with you every day has spoiled me. I don't want to leave you."

She was silent. She didn't want to leave him, either.

"Aren't you going to fix me some breakfast? You don't want me to go out into the cold, brutal jungle to

face the ravening corporate maneuverings on an empty
stomach, do you?''

"No." She got out of bed and went for her robe. He
stopped her and held her against him.

Her throat worked and she clutched at him. He
patted her bottom. "I'm glad you'll be here when I get
back.''

She didn't look at him, but put on her robe and
went to the kitchen. She washed her hands, fixed him
bacon and eggs, toast and jam, juice and coffee.

He told her about the other two companies while he
ate. She didn't listen; she watched him. He was excited over the prospect, and was stimulated in anticipation of matching wits. He was typically a warrior,
who was facing a battle of another kind.

When he got to the door, he held her and hugged
her again. "I hate to leave you." It was lip service. Oh,
he did want to stay, but he'd been almost as much of
a prisoner as she those last ten days.

He said, "Miss me."

She raised wet eyes to his. He was delighted with her
tears.

He hugged her tightly. "When I get back tonight,
we'll make some plans. Okay?" He kissed her long
and lovely. Then he patted her bottom again, caressed her here and there, grinned as he sighed in regret and he left.

She was dressed and had packed one small bag,
when the phone rang. She answered it hesitantly. She
wasn't sure she could handle it, if the caller should be
Luke. It was Mac.

"Hi, Georgia. I just thought I should tell you that
Luke is having your car delivered back to you this

morning. He thought you might like to drive it again, after being cooped up so long. And he suggested the grocery store could be an ideal goal. He wants steaks tonight.''

''Yes.''

''Georgia, for the last ten days I've been telling Luke to be careful of you. And I told him to tell you about the Molly Q on Saturday, but now I've got to tell you—be careful of him.''

''I haven't been here by choice.''

''I know. But I've never seen Luke like this over a woman. You have to pay attention and not trifle with him. He has a very bad case on you.''

''He thinks I know Herb.''

''It was a natural conclusion, when he found you with the folder on the Molly Q.''

''I don't know Herb. I've never met him. I don't even know anyone named Herb.''

''Yes. Well. I just wanted to let you know that you ought to take it easy on Luke.''

''Yes.''

''You're in a funny mood. Are you all right?''

''I'll get the steak.''

''Okay. I want you to meet Penny—''

But she interrupted. ''There's someone at the door.''

''It's probably the car jockey. Peek first. Make him identify himself.''

''Mac.''

''Yeah?''

''I'm glad you're Luke's friend. Goodbye.''

* * *

There wasn't anyone at the door. She just couldn't talk to Mac about Luke. She gathered all her things and organized them.

When the doorbell did ring, it was the car jockey. Georgia went down to inspect her car, and it was green. He had really had it painted. It was a lovely green. But she looked at it and she wasn't pleased. The color was exactly what she would have chosen, but she didn't like it that he'd just gone ahead and had it done.

She asked the car jockey, "How much would that paint job cost?"

"It was the deluxe and it had to be at least four hundred."

"Let me thank you for bringing it over to me." She held out two bills.

"It's already taken care of. Thanks, anyway." He grinned, got into a waiting pickup and was gone.

She would leave. She could move out now. The car was there. Everything she owned was up in the apartment. She had the time to haul it down, pack it into the car and she would leave.

But first she went to a bank and cashed a check for four hundred dollars, crippling her account. She went to a grocery and bought him a huge steak that looked as if it was something thrown against the bars of a lion's cage, and then she went back to the apartment.

She put the cash with the car receipt on his desk under the edge of the desk phone. She put the steak on a platter and poured lemon juice over it and sliced onions on it before she seasoned it to marinate in the refrigerator. It would be very tender and delicious for him.

She breathed a little roughly, but she didn't cry yet. She changed into scruffy clothes, pulled her boxes from his study and put both animals into that room and closed the door, blocking it so that Minny couldn't free them. Then she carried all that stuff down the stairs in several trips and packed her car.

She took down the pictures and left the nails in the wall. That was the way her heart felt: full of nails and scorched from being too close to his fires. His eyes had promised she'd be safe that close to him. They had lied.

She removed all other evidence of her captivity. Then she opened his study door and groped for Minny.

It took some time for her to realize it wasn't the dog that was making Minny elusive. Minny didn't want to leave. And it was that which finally made her cry.

Minny put her back up and hissed, and she even growled! "Oh, Minny!" Georgia wailed. But the cat wasn't swayed.

Everything else was packed. Carrying her reluctant struggling cat and weeping, Georgia went around the apartment, seeing Luke everywhere. She finally wrote a note which wasn't too coherent.

This money is for the car. It isn't rent for the last ten days. I feel I've more than paid my way. I don't know anyone named Herb!

She didn't sign it. How many other people had spent the last ten days there? She looked at the note. Her writing was ghastly. She cried some more. Minny growled low in her throat and struggled. Mutt followed her around, watching her. He knew.

She really hated to leave the dog there, all alone. She put Minny in the car and slammed the door. She went back, fetched Mutt and took him for a nice walk. The dog enjoyed being out, but Georgia cried.

Taking the dog back to the apartment, she added a P.S. "The dog went outside at—" It was already ten. "—ten."

The dog appeared to wrinkle up the wisps that seemed like eyebrows, and he whined a little over her leaving him. She hesitated. Then remembering the doubled security, she opened the sliding door onto the balcony for him, and then she left.

She leaked tears all the way from Indianapolis to Cleveland, where the traffic distracted her long enough until she was almost to the little town that was home. She had a dreadful headache.

She drove into the yard, with the other family cars, the pickup and a John Deere tractor, and she looked around. She was home.

The Browns' enormous house was on the edge of their tiny town. Her parents had bought it at an auction when they were first married. It had been abandoned. Of all the family, only Georgia could see the place with clear eyes and realize the people who had abandoned it had been smart.

But the Browns loved it. It was a house to love. It was big, sprawling and in need of paint, in need of almost everything except love. It had come with almost ten worthless acres. Land good for nothing but kids and pets. There were dogs, a cow, any number of cats, but actually about four.

No one had ever ridden the pony. It didn't like to be ridden.

There were the inevitable chickens who were as un-disciplined and individual as everything else around, and the Browns had to constantly hunt for their nests to find the eggs. They had a nanny goat left over from the time Felicia Brown had thought goat cheese was rather arty. The animals were well-cared-for, brushed and clean.

The children were also reasonably clean and tidy. The Browns only had five offspring of their own, but they seemed to continually collect other people's children. In that house, there were all those rooms to fill, and the additional children didn't appear to bother anyone.

Her father was an ex-Navy man and had spent some time in the boxing ring. He was considerably older than his wife. He had a car dealership and he was a genius with motors and ancient furnaces, antique plumbing and mending things. He could fix anything. He could cook, he adored Felicia, and he had a magic touch with children. He was called Salty.

As Georgia sat in her newly green car with her cat and all her worldly possessions, it was her father who first came out on the porch and stood there watching her.

Then her mother drifted out anxiously.

Georgia opened the car door, and Minny spat some disparaging sound at Georgia before she hopped down to weave her graceful way to Felicia.

Her father wobbled the railing to test its strength, and finding it stable, leaned against it and waited.

They knew something was wrong. They knew what she'd been through with Phillip's death, but they had thought she was finally all right. What had happened over there in Indianapolis?

Georgia pried herself out of her green car and looked around the beloved yard, the leaning barn and her very dear parents. She started to cry again. She looked at her parents and cried like a child. A twenty-eight-year-old woman was bawling like a ten-year-old.

Ten

Georgia's parents met her at the bottom of the steps and all three enfolded each other.

Her dad rasped, "How bad is it? Do I have to bend anybody?"

That's what he always said when someone cried and he didn't know why.

Georgia sobbed, "I love a man who's through with women."

Her dad scoffed, "No man's that dumb."

"And he thinks another man sent me to spy on him, and he doesn't believe me." None of which made a whole lot of sense.

In her best "Raggs's mother" voice, which trembled with emotion, Felicia said, "Oh, darling!"

As usual, they went to the kitchen. It was a very large and welcoming room. There was a wood stove cleaned and blackened for the coming winter, a round oak table, extended into an oval with its added leaves so it easily seated a dozen people. Against the bank of windows, step benches held pots of herbs and flowers. The pots of begonias took turns being centerpieces for the table.

Georgia was given a cosseting cup of tea with some of Helen's milk. Helen was their cow. She had very large long-lashed brown eyes like Felicia's aunt and was named for her aunt, who hadn't felt especially honored.

Just as Georgia was ready to launch into a long and incoherently rambling dissertation on her life and times, Felicia asked, "Could you possibly take the role of the twelve-year-old tonight? She has chicken pox."

"In the play?"

"No, she really has them. If we bind your chest and braid your hair, I'm sure you could pass."

"Mother—"

"We have been out of our minds trying to solve this. For most of the performance you can be offstage and shout your lines while you read them, but with the dog, Raggs, as offstage sounds, too, it's asking a bit much of the audience. I can just see the reviewer saying, 'Why didn't they all just hide behind the curtain?' or something equally asinine. You know, just because he's from Cleveland, you'd think he was from the *New York Times!* Insufferable."

"I could bend him a little for you," Salty volunteered in his rasping voice.

"No, darling, but I do appreciate the mental image it gives me, and that's very satisfying." Felicia then turned to Georgia. "What do you think, Baby? It would only be a few lines, and when it's essential that you be onstage, I could turn my back to the audience and feed your lines to you. You would save the show!"

"Oh, Mother—" Georgia wailed.

"It could distract you. Give you something else to think about. Don't you agree, Francis?" She was the only one who dared to call him that.

"You're always right."

"Daddy!"

"Stand up, dear. I think I have a cotton shift that would be perfect as a kind of jumper for you that would look reasonably childish and cover your figure well enough if we bind you properly."

"I can't."

And the rasping voice supplied, "No Brown ever heard the word 'can't' or uses it."

"That's true," her mother agreed.

Just about then, since there was an hour's time difference, it was after four o'clock at the Montana Electronics Company, Inc. in Indianapolis, Indiana. Luke was frowning at the wall as the phone in his hand rang yet again. Where was she? How long did it take to go out and buy some steaks? The car had been delivered at eight-thirty, and she hadn't been there since.

A very strange feeling gripped Luke. He went back to the meeting, jerked a hand at Mac and backed out the door to wait in the hall.

"What's up?"

"I can't get hold of Georgia," Luke said. "I've been calling her since about ten this morning, and she doesn't answer. I have a bad feeling about this."

Mac discounted that. "She probably went to a movie or apartment hunting, or shopping. Women never sit by the phone and wait for someone to call them. They gad about all over the place. You'll be smart to take home some deli food for supper to-night." Then Mac urged, "We'd better get back. This is going perfectly. I wouldn't have dreamed it would be handed to us this way. You're good." Mac grinned at Luke.

"You've done most of the talking. You're doing great. I've got to find out about Georgia. I just wanted you to know I'm leaving. I'll be in touch."

"Huh?"

But Luke was gone.

It was two days before he drove into the Browns' yard. The house was enormous. All the windows were open on the summer day, and there was a ball game going on over in a pasture, with a wide range of ages in the participants. They ignored the new arrival.

Luke was tired. He got out of the car and looked around. There was a great elm, which had obviously survived the Dutch elm plague that had wiped out so many trees in the Midwest. It shaded the whole side yard and its collection of vehicles.

The house needed paint. The porches were tilted a bit, but there were two padded swings, white-pointed wicker chairs, rockers and two tables, and great tubs of petunias. There were man-size rubber plants, rush rugs, and the setting lured people to sit and rest a while.

On beyond a fence, there was a cow watching him with some interest. There were chickens scratching in the yard, and a dog lying, panting in the shade, who didn't bother to challenge him.

Minny came from the edge of the porch and gave him a tiny mew. Then she jumped into his arms, sure of her welcome.

She purred for him, lifting her head for his petting. "Where is she, Minny?" Luke asked the tiny cat, then looked up to see the big man in the doorway. "With Minny here, this has to be Browns'?" Luke questioned, holding the cat.

"You gotta be Luke." The great shoulders, the cauliflower ear, and the rasping voice told Luke of the man's boxing background. He'd taken too many blows to his throat and that had altered his voice.

Salty opened the screen and offered his big ham hand to Luke. Shifting Minny, Luke took the man's hand and braced himself for a crippling grip. But Salty Brown didn't need to prove anything. His clasp was firm and kind. Luke saw he wasn't a young man anymore, and he wore a tea towel around his trim hips as an apron.

"I'm her father."

Luke took a big, relaxing breath. He said, "There are more than a few Browns around."

"Yeah."

"She is here?"

Salty smiled. To Luke, there was only one "she" in the world.

"Where did you get a name like Montana?"

"Probably, back some time ago, there was a drifter with something to hide who adopted the state for his name."

With that, Salty laughed a wheezing rasp and said, "Come on in. We'll go to the kitchen. I'm cooking." He gave no excuse nor explanation.

The kitchen was like Hollywood's dream of a farm kitchen. Luke stood and looked around, lifting his head to inhale.

"Want a beer?"

"Thanks, but I have to keep my wits about me."

Salty smiled. "How about some cucumber soup?"

Luke vividly recalled Georgia's, but gamely said, "That would be fine."

And Salty turned away to hide his smile. Georgia had told them everything.

Luke set Minny on the floor and petted down her back to smooth her fur comfortably. Salty noted that. Then Luke sat at the big oval table and carefully tasted the chilled soup. With some surprise he said, "It's delicious!"

Salty leaned his backside against the counter and smiled. "It just takes time to learn things."

Luke knew Georgia's father wasn't talking about cucumber soup. But like soup, it takes time to learn to live in this world, and it takes time to make a relationship work. Luke was learning.

On cue, Felicia wafted in like a slender flower bending with the breeze. Luke rose as she said, "I'm her mother. You may call me Felicia." And she smiled sweetly as "Raggs's mother" would smile at a nice young man.

She sat across from Luke, so he wouldn't have to turn his head to look at her. She told him to go on with his soup. And she watched him shrewdly.

"Georgia told me you're an actress," Luke mentioned nicely, to encourage her to talk to him.

Was she really shy? She turned her head a little before she appeared to summon the courage to modestly admit it: "Yes."

"How's the play going? If I remember, this is about Lassie?"

"That's the family's name for the play. It's really named *Raggs to the Rescue*. It's broadly done. Since we don't have five talented dogs who look alike and are expert actors, we have a sound track of local dogs. Mrs. Potts's Terry who whines *all* the time, and Mr. Lennon's Leo—Leo Lennon!" Felicia briefly lifted eloquent eyes to the kitchen ceiling. "Leo's bark is formidable! And Cassie Templeton's Midget—who is predictably humongous!—we have his snarl. Beautiful snarl. He lifts the hair right off your head.

"But Raggs is only seen twice. He's such a stupid, friendly dog. So we allow him onstage right at the beginning, and again for the curtain. Georgia has a part." Felicia paused and watched Luke with deceptive blandness.

That Georgia would be in the play so soon shook Luke. He raised stark eyes to Felicia and asked, "She's in the play?" She could walk away from him, come home and go immediately into a lighthearted play?

Felicia smiled, like a cat with a canary, and elaborated more kindly, "Our twelve-year-old star came down with chicken pox. Imagine that! She's a brilliant actress and is devastated. We only comforted her by promising we'd put on *The Bad Seed*." Felicia shuddered delicately. "I shall, of course, play her mother.

"She is quite ill. And although the part isn't crucial, it is germane. So when Georgia showed up so providentially—" Felicia spared a flicking, droll glance at Luke "—we convinced her to take on the role."

There was some silence.

"A twelve-year-old?" Luke tilted his head and gave Felicia a brief, disbelieving look.

"In braids, and with her chest bound."

"She came home and just agreed to do the play?" His tone was mild, he kept his stare on his plate and he didn't move.

The rasping voice of Georgia's father provided the reply: "—bawling all the way."

So Luke was able to continue with the cucumber soup, not quite so discouraged.

Salty's rasp coaxed, "Drink a little beef broth, Felicia. You need your strength."

"I can't. You know that."

"It's several hours before you go onstage. Some of it will stay with you. Try just a little. I worry about you."

She looked perfectly healthy to Luke. Mr. Brown spoiled his wife. "How did you two meet?" Luke looked up at Felicia, then over to Salty.

And it was he who gave the answer. "I was Navy. A twenty-year man. Went through World War Two and after Korea I retired and came here. It was far enough away from the water. In one play they needed some muscles on the stage, and Felicia was the understudy. She fell insanely in love with me, compromised me and my parents made her marry me to save my good name."

Felicia slumped. "I've spent thirty years trying to make him truthful."

The rasp said, "You are the most beautiful woman in all the world."

She straightened and smiled ethereally. "There is hope for you, after all."

His eyes moving from one to the other, Luke listened to their easy teasing, and he began to reevaluate his understanding of Georgia, their child. One thing was clear: they gave complete loyalty and total commitment.

During that time, other people came through the house bent on their own errands. Felicia moved Luke out onto a side porch as kids came in, washed their hands, grinned and set the table.

"A job for everyone?" Luke inquired of Felicia.

"Organization. He was Navy, you know."

Salty brought her a little pudding. With her small silver spoon, she played with it, eating it all eventually and not realizing it. Salty watched every bite.

"Sit here, darling," she told her husband, "it's cooler."

And he allowed her to adjust the pillow.

"There's Georgia's car," said Salty. "If you go through the house to the front door, she'll come in that way."

Luke gave a brief nod and hurried inside as her parents exchanged a look.

Georgia got her weary bones out of her green car and tiredly pushed back her lank hair. She wondered who was visiting who had a car like Luke's. How cruel. She had never learned to check car license plates, so it was just a car. She looked mournfully out over the fields away from town and groaned over the thought she had to go onstage again that night. How did she get into these things?

Her family.

They knew she needed distracting, and they went at it with a will. She wondered if the twelve-year-old she was replacing was really sick. Felicia said chicken pox, another had said a cold and someone else had mentioned a dead relative.

She drooped up the steps, across the wide porch and opened the screen door. In the minute it took for her eyes to adjust to the shaded interior of the house, she came electrically alive. She straightened and gasped, and her eyes found the looming cause. *It was Luke and he was there!*

Her eyes went over him, greedily noting everything. He was whole, he was tired, his suit coat was off, his shirt unbuttoned two buttons, his sleeves rolled up twice. His shoes were dusty. His trousers were soft. Minny sat next to him.

He was watching her and his own eyes hungrily covered her. He was standing at the foot of their grand stair, his forearm resting on the swirled newel post. He said, "Do you have any idea how many Browns there are 'near' Cleveland?" And his voice was a low growl.

She watched, fascinated, as if a mirage spoke to her. She figured she'd finally flipped and conjured him up. How amazing her mind could choose exactly what he would more than likely actually say! If he was really there.

"Do you know what it was like for me to get to that apartment, worried sick because you hadn't answered the phone, and find everything gone? Only nails left all over the walls showed that you'd ever been there! How could you do that to me?''

''To *you?* How many times did I tell you I didn't know any Herb and you didn't believe me?'' Now she was replying to the illusion! That proved she had gone bonkers.

''Yeah? He said to tell you hello!''

''*He* said? Who said?''

''Herb. We talked.''

''He lied. You think I was there because he sent me, but it—''

''I told him the whole story. He was fascinated.''

''—isn't true. I am sick and tired of trying to convince you I am telling the truth.''

''I know.''

''Unless the four hundred isn't enough for the car?''

''I brought the money back to you. The paint job was a gift.''

''I can't accept gifts from a stranger.''

He was indignant. ''Do you consider me a stranger?''

She turned her face aside. ''I can't even recall your name.'' Then she gave him a snooty glance. ''What did you do with Mutt?''

''He's out in the car.''

''He'll die of the heat out there!'' she exclaimed. ''Bring him inside.''

''I believe this is about the way this whole affair began. But it was Minny instead of a dog.'' His deep voice was very tender.

He had left the newel post and moved almost imperceptibly nearer, so that she wasn't so overwhelmed by him. But she realized he was closer, and she was leaning forward just a little. "Did you say you knew?"

"Hmm?" He blinked.

"A while ago, when I said I didn't know Herb, did you say you knew that?"

"Yes."

"When did you know?"

"Almost immediately."

She frowned, as she worked on that sentence. "I'll help with Mutt. The dogs accept cats fairly well, but a strange dog has to be introduced."

While they were doing that, Salty rang the bell for dinner, and automatically Georgia showed Luke where to wash.

"Did you leave me because I didn't tell you about the Molly Q sinking? I was afraid, if you knew, you'd leave me."

"No. Because you asked me if Herb was as good as you. You offended me. You made me sound like a bed-hopper. I told you I didn't know any Herb."

"I was sure you didn't and I only meant to tease, to make you say I was a good lover. I would never try to offend you."

She was silent.

Luke wanted to hold her. He wasn't sure she'd allow it. He asked, "How's your arm?"

"Just fine. You can hardly see the marks any more."

"Let me see." So when he had her arm in his hands, he could kiss the phantom marks, then he could kiss her. She cried, and he comforted her. He kissed her some more, and she kissed him back. He urged, "Forgive me."

She had to swallow first. Forgive him? How angry could she still be when she was willingly locked in his arms and kissing him back? "When did you know I didn't know Herb?"

"That first day."

She reared back indignantly. "The whole time?"

"Now, how was I going to keep you there, if you didn't feel mistrusted and threatened? We had a hell of a time setting it all up!"

"You set it ... up?"

"I walked into that conference room and there you were. I locked the door so you couldn't get away. I had to think of some way to keep you there. I knew you had to be traveling, because that's the way couriers work.

"When I came back to an empty conference room, I almost panicked! I thought I'd lost you. Then I found you looking at the blueprint for cattle pens at the ranch. Inspiration hit like lightning."

"Cattle pens? But Mac?"

"Mac is an old and trusted friend. He will go along with anything reasonably honest. He damned near blew it with calling you Sweet Georgia Brown. Did you tumble to our knowing exactly who you were by then?"

"There wasn't any Molly Q?"

"The blueprints had nothing to do with the experiments we were conducting in electronics. That is fact."

"You *tricked* me!"

"No, no. We organized you. I kept you available." He was surprised she didn't appear to understand.

She was braced against him, by then, and indignant. "What about the invader?"

"Apparently a genuine burglar! He was a surprise. I scared the bloody hell out of him." Luke grinned.

"And Herb was never interested in seeing me? He was never a threat?"

"He could have been, but he's more subtle. I needed something to hassle you with, so I'd have a reason to keep you."

"You made all that up? About Herb?"

He grinned. "Yeah. I did wonder a time or two. Your sketchbook. Then the burglar..."

"You dreadful man!"

"And, honey, about that hundred thousand. Would you take it a dollar down and a dollar a week? That's about the only way I can make payment."

She sassed, "I need either a lump sum—"

"Now, there wasn't anything in the contract about *how* it was to be paid."

"Or compensation. And we never actually had any real contract."

He grinned at her. "There were any number of times you could have yelled or escaped. When your dad called, when the florist came. From the balcony. At night when I slept. Why didn't you?"

"When you came into the conference room, I was so shaken that I couldn't really reply coherently."

"Why not?"

"You made me want to drag you off to my lair."

"Women feel that sort of reaction?"

"We never admit it."

"So you only pretended to resist?"

"No. That was real. I was scared of you."

"Not of *me*? How could you be afraid of me?"

"You could have been married and off-limits to another woman."

"That was the first thing I found out about you. Parker checked your driver's license. I knew I had to have you. I have heard fables of men falling in love with a magic princess, but I never thought it would happen to me. Can you love me?"

"How can you think I don't? I would never have stayed past that first night, even in the storm. I could have left then. I knew I was safe when you rented the cot. You were darling."

"I thought so, too."

"And you were so sweet about my cooking. Daddy's a genius cook . . . my God, they're waiting for us to eat!"

But the parents hadn't waited. Being lovers themselves, they had allowed everyone else to go ahead with the meal.

Salty fixed the tardy couple's plates from the leftovers, and the two sat at the kitchen table. The superb fare was wasted on their distraction.

Then Georgia took Luke out to show him about the place, and through the big old house, with all its nooks and crannies. She even took him up in the attic, where they clutched each other with feverish and frantic kisses.

So Luke got to go to the play that night, and he was charmed by them all. What a bunch of hams. And he watched Georgia and her mother in their exchanges and he smiled the entire time.

It was a while before they were married. They had to wait until the play closed. Luke wasn't sure about that, but Felicia put her hand to her forehead and closed her eyes. Then Salty took a firm stand on the issue.

Luke stayed at the Browns' house and settled in quite well. He took his turn pitching for the home team, then switched and pitched for the Outcasts. That group was the other half of the family. He taught the younger ones to hold, throw and catch a football. That was automatic, but he also tried milking the patient cow, forked hay for the pony and gathered eggs from the hidden hens' nests. It was a different world.

And he stole time to lean Georgia against a wall or a door or a post and kiss her until her brain whirled, but someone always came along and hooted and laughed and yelled to the other, "Hey! They're *smooching!*"

Georgia's brother, Bob, returned from Boston, jobless, divorced and disgruntled. He was quiet and rarely smiled. He was suffering. The younger ones made Bob play ball, too, but his heart wasn't in it, and his mind was on something else.

By the time the play closed to rave reviews, Luke's parents had returned from the Lake Michigan cruise and were absorbed into the big Brown house as if they'd always lived there. The Montanas knew quite a few of the key people in Cleveland, all of whom came to the play, brought friends for the next performance, packed the theater and entered into the farce with invigorating enthusiasm.

And Mrs. Montana knew the reviewer—who owed her a favor.

The wedding took place in the clapboard church just down the road from the theater. It was at midnight, after the play's final curtain. All the theater guests who chose to, came to the wedding and it, too, was packed.

Mac was best man, so Georgia finally could meet his wife, Penny. She was an organized, practical person, and the two women liked each other on sight. That was fortunate.

Herb sent a silver tray and his regrets.

The reception, of course, was at the Browns' house and all the windows and doors were open to the sultry summer night. Salty baked the wedding cake, and since he knew how things generally turned out in that household, there was ample food and the punch had punch.

Bob solemnly helped at whatever his dad said for him to do. He kissed his sister and very seriously shook hands with Luke. He didn't dance.

There was a spinet piano that collected the usual friends who were musicians and came prepared to play. The Oriental rugs were rolled away, and there was dancing. It was the usual Brown party, noisy, and fun with friendly laughter.

"I never in my life thought I'd hesitate to leave my own wedding reception," Luke told Georgia.

"Let's not. It's our party. Let's enjoy it. We have the rest of our lives."

"Honey. Your dad gave me a check for our honeymoon. I don't know how to handle this. They can't afford to give us all that money. They won't let my folks even help with the food, and look at all our relatives here."

Georgia kissed him and replied, "Daddy could buy you twice over. He doesn't let anyone know that, because mother loves it, right here, and to have her life just this way. If they started living too well, or doing things differently, their friends wouldn't be as comfortable with them. They choose to be like everyone else. This way, no one robs them, no one plagues them for money. No one bothers them. They get to live their lives exactly the way they want."

Luke grinned and ruefully shook his head. "Dad and I have spent most of the time here trying to figure a way to help them get the house painted. Mother said to leave them alone. They might be pride-bound, but that your mother's jewelry was excellent and her dresses fit perfectly.

"She also mentioned the rugs are genuine, the crystal pieces are put in the dishwasher, and the sterling is loose in the kitchen drawer and used every meal. She said we shouldn't mention money."

Georgia explained: "Generally, it doesn't go this long between house paintings. The friend who does the painting for them, fell three years ago and he still isn't quite ready to get back to work. They're waiting on him. Does it bother you? The way the place looks?"

"I believe they are brilliant."

"I think you are," she told him. "Have I mentioned that I love you?"

"You never did."

"I have, too!"

"Refresh my memory."

"Oh, Luke, how could I be so lucky to have you love me?"

"Clean living? God owes you?"

"You beast. Kiss me."

"I have decided my kisses are worth a dollar each. That way, if I work at it, I can get out of debt to you by kissing you all the time. How long will it take to give you a hundred thousand kisses?"

"You never did pay me back for the hamburgers I bought you that first day!"

"I could just add it to your tab?"

"Good grief!"

"For better or worse, remember."

"I love you."

"Oh, Georgia, how I love you!" He held her there in the midst of the revelry, and he kissed her thoroughly.

She knew he truly loved her. Those warm fires he'd used to draw her to him weren't just fires of passion. They were the fires of his love. And they would never harm her. They would warm her, protect her, and light her way through the rest of their lives.

*　*　*　*　*

SILHOUETTE·INTIMATE·MOMENTS®

IT'S TIME TO MEET
THE MARSHALLS!

In 1986, bestselling author Kristin James wrote A VERY SPECIAL FAVOR for the Silhouette Intimate Moments line. Hero Adam Marshall quickly became a reader favorite, and ever since then, readers have been asking for the stories of his two brothers, Tag and James. At last your prayers have been answered!

In August, look for THE LETTER OF THE LAW (IM #393), James Marshall's story. If you missed youngest brother Tag's story, SALT OF THE EARTH (IM #385), you can order it by following the directions below. And, as our very special favor to you, we'll be reprinting A VERY SPECIAL FAVOR this September. Look for it in special displays wherever you buy books.

Silhouette Books®

Silhouette Special Edition

presents

SONNY'S GIRLS

by Emilie Richards, Celeste Hamilton and Erica Spindler

They had been Sonny's girls, irresistibly drawn to the charismatic high school football hero. Ten years later, none could forget the night that changed their lives forever.

In July—
ALL THOSE YEARS AGO by Emilie Richards (SSE #684)
Meredith Robbins had left town in shame. Could she ever banish the past and reach for love again?

In August—
DON'T LOOK BACK by Celeste Hamilton (SSE #690)
Cyndi Saint was Sonny's steady. Ten years later, she remembered only his hurtful parting words....

In September—
LONGER THAN... by Erica Spindler (SSE #696)
Bubbly Jennifer Joyce was everybody's friend. But nobody knew the secret longings she felt for bad boy Ryder Hayes....

Coming Soon

Fashion A Whole New You. Win a sensual adventurous trip for two to Hawaii via American Airlines®, a brand-new Ford Explorer 4 × 4 and a $2,000 Fashion Allowance.

Plus, special free gifts* are yours to Fashion A Whole New You.

From September through November, you can take part in this exciting opportunity from Silhouette.

Watch for details in September.

* with proofs-of-purchase, plus postage and handling